SECRETS OF THE VOLKOVS

Ellie Jay

Independently Published

CONTENTS

Title Page

Copyright

Family   1

Preparing   10

The Mission Begins   18

Dariya   25

The Volkovs   31

Planning   38

The First Secret   46

Dariya's Secret   52

Evidence   58

The 'Moving In' Mission   63

The Attack   71

Rescue?   77

Aftermath   82

Hiding Out   88

The Traitor   94

Escaping Yaroslavl   102

Dmitri and the Chase   107

News   112

The Fall and The Wedding   122

Preparation   127

The Volkovs Invade   132

Fighting to The Death   138

The End of a Life   147

Dariya's World After Antonin   153

Nikolina's New Life   160

Hiding the Past   166

Books In This Series   173

H

Th

Esc

Dm

Big N

The C

CONTENTS

Title Page

Copyright

Family 1

Preparing 10

The Mission Begins 18

Dariya 25

The Volkovs 31

Planning 38

The First Secret 46

Dariya's Secret 52

Evidence 58

The 'Moving In' Mission 63

The Attack 71

Rescue? 77

Aftermath 82

Hiding Out 88

The Traitor 94

Escaping Yaroslavl 102

Dmitri and the Chase 107

Big News 112

The Call and The Wedding 122

Preparation   127
The Volkovs Invade   132
Fighting to The Death   138
The End of a Life   147
Dariya's World After Antonin   153
Nikolina's New Life   160
Hiding the Past   166
Books In This Series   173

FAMILY

Nikolina Moroz shuffled her notes in one hand and the frying pan in the other. She was trying to cook up a hearty breakfast for her family, but her eyes were fixed rigidly on the paperwork in front of her.

Shaking his head despairingly from his seat at the nearby dining table is Alexander, her little brother."Sis, chill! I'm sure this case of yours will be fine, even if you tear your eyes away from your notes for a second!" he tried to reassure her, seeing that his older sister was very stressed.

"I wish I had your confidence," Nikolina groaned in reply, still not looking up from her work.

"Well, you better lend her some fast, Sasha, or our breakfast's gonna set the house on fire!" Another flippant voice chipped in as Ekaterina, the duo's younger sister ran into the room with a bag slung casually over her shoulder and plonked herself down on a chair beside her brother.

"Katya, enough! Now is no time to tease your sister!" the scolding, fatherly tones of Mr. Ilya Moroz, their single father and a fearsome parent who often forgot to reserve his sharpest tones for the criminals he dealt with as the local chief of police, thundered out across the room.

He saw Katya's frozen expression and softened a bit. "I know, I know, you were only joking. But Lina's a little busy right now..." he pointed out.

Nikolina was still intently focused on her work.

"Lina, your work ethic has been wonderful since you started on this case, but you always do so well at work. I'm sure you know what you're doing without all this," he gestured at her paperwork, "And if you can at least put it down and put breakfast on the table, then we can get these two sorted out," he pointed at his other two children, "You know Katya can't afford to be late to college again."

He turned a sharp, emerald-eyed glare on his youngest and most troublesome child, before glancing over at his son. "And Sasha... Well, what are you planning to get up to today, Sasha?" he paused, questioning the young man.

The response was an absent-minded shrug, followed by Sasha beginning to explain to his father, "No idea. Detective Honesko said he wouldn't need me this week..." he trailed off at this point, giving a little sigh.

This made Ilya sigh too and survey his children thoughtfully.

Nikolina, or Lina as she was affectionately known, was the eldest at twenty-eight. She was a pretty young woman, favouring her late mother in looks, as she bore Elena's long, blonde hair. It was straight and fell down over her shoulders, though this morning it was wound up on her head in a tight bun.

She was also tall and slender, with a thin face and pointed features. Again, she took after her mother here. Elena had always reminded him of an elf or pixie from a fairy story. He smiled fondly. Nikolina's resemblance to her mother always took him back to a happier time.

But she was not unlike him, either. She had deep-set emerald-green eyes as well, and she had definitely inherited certain important values of his. Her strong, almost devoted work ethic put him very much in mind of himself, as did her sense of justice.

That, along with her three years of hard work at a local legal firm, told him that, despite her obvious stress, her first solo case as a lawyer would turn out just fine.

But right now, she seemed a little distracted by her family. Of course. In the nine years since her mother died, she had taken on the duty of looking after her younger siblings, to the point where it was a habit for her to make the family meals and take care of their home.

He was deeply grateful for that. It allowed him to keep working as hard as his job required and still know that everything was taken care of.

Still, now of all times, it wasn't right. He turned back to Sasha, "If you're not doing anything, then help Lina out!" he told him.

The younger man got up and took the frying pan from his sister, who immediately wandered away dreamily, still clutching her papers.

Sasha soon finished making breakfast and started dishing it up for everyone. As he did so, his father's thoughts turned to the middle child.

Alexander, better known to the family as Sasha, also favoured his mother. He had short, wavy blond hair and her wide, baby blue eyes. Though he had inherited his father's strong build.

The twenty-four-year-old was at a bit of a loose end at the moment. He was a recent criminology graduate but had quit the first job his father had lined up for him - In the police force, of course - because he had a very unique way of doing things, by following his instincts, not necessarily the rulebook.

Often, Sasha was right in these cases. He had a great arrest rate in his time as a cop, and he was compassionate in his way of administering justice. But he had felt he was putting his father in an awkward position. It looked bad if the chief's son could break the rules and still have a great record.

Ilya hadn't thought of it that way, but Sasha had made up his mind, so he had moved on. Out of a sense of duty to help his considerate son out, Ilya had found him a second job, helping out an old friend who ran a private detective's firm.

But apparently business was slack right now, and it was getting the young man down. Yet, Ilya felt sure that would be short-lived. Sasha had his whole life ahead of him. He was well-qualified, with his father's sense of justice, his mother's compassion and his own sharp instincts. Things could only get better.

Right now, the man in question was busy with breakfast. He placed a plate down in front of his father then handed one to his younger sister.

As Ekaterina took it, Sasha turned to watch Nikolina wander towards the stairs with her gaze still on the papers she was carrying. "Sis? Aren't you going to eat?" he called after her in evident concern.

Ekaterina shook her head. "She's not paying any attention, bro. Before long she's gonna walk into something.... It'll be the only way she'll look up," she thoughtfully commented on her older sister's activities before diving into her breakfast.

Ilya sighed again. Then, of course, there was Ekaterina. Katya was sixteen, the baby of the family. She stood shorter than her siblings' by at least half a foot and had slightly darker blonde hair than the others' platinum tones, closer to her father's own locks. It bounced down her back in wild waves.

The wild hair and her sparkling green eyes reflected much of her nature. She was loud, flippant and full of mischievous cheer. He wasn't sure where she got that attitude from. His wife had been a bright soul, certainly. He often struggled to begrudge Katya the trouble she caused him because her smile put him in mind of Elena.

But Elena had never been so... over the top. He despaired of Katya's endless energy, wondering how she would ever be persuaded to settle down and find herself a steady job.

Not that that seemed very relevant right now, seeing as she had no idea what she wanted to do with her life. She was currently enrolled on a writing course at a local community college, but her plans after that were vague, and she was more focused on having a good time with her friends than actually attending and passing the course.

Still, she was certainly a unique soul. He could only hope she would settle down a little.

It was here that Ilya's thoughts came to an abrupt end. Sasha was beginning to panic, chasing after his sister worriedly.

Ilya stood up and strode over, stopping him with a simple hand on the shoulder. "You sit down and eat your breakfast. I'll go and talk to her. See if I can get her to re-join us... and I'll fetch Antonin down as well," he assured Sasha, who began to head back to his seat.

Antonin. He brought Ilya back to his family as he set off up the stairs, musing on the fifth, final and unofficial family member.

The young man had first entered his life as a colleague, eight years earlier. A trainee police officer with a fiery temper and stubborn attitude, who he suspected had just joined the force in search of an adventure.Antonin had been a huge red flag to the serious dedicated police chief.

So, he had appointed himself the man's mentor. That was seven years ago, and now, well, Antonin was still Antonin, of course. But, he had calmed down somewhat and gained a new respect for his job Even if Ilya suspected that he still craved adventure more than anything else.

What was more important, though, was the fact that the two men had somehow become good friends, despite their differences.

They had begun to visit each other informally, away from the office. That was something Ilya rarely did, and it was also how Antonin met Nikolina.

Ilya wasn't sure he believed in love at first sight, but his student and his daughter clearly did. They had met a year and a few months ago and now Antonin had enough of his things in Nikolina's room that he might as well live there. He certainly slept over often enough.

With that in mind, he headed there in search of the young couple.

Meanwhile, Antonin was resting on his girlfriend's bed looking out of the window as the traffic crawled past. Even this early on a late spring morning, the Moscow suburb was busy.

Watching the cars helped him think. He needed to think right now, as he was carefully considering his future.He was unaware of Ilya's thoughts about him being an unofficial member of the family, but he certainly wanted to be a part of the Moroz family.

He loved their house, which had soon become his second home.Estranged from his own family, his living options consisted of a tiny apartment several miles away,n inconvenient, cramped place with no entertainment,Or the Moroz house, where there was plenty of space. It was an easy trip into work every morning via Ilya's car, and most importantly, there were other people.

Nikolina was his favourite companion there, of course. He loved her to bits. it certainly helped that he had grown close to her father and was beginning to get to know her siblings too, though they were still more or less strangers. It was a start at least. One day... One day, they might feel like family.

In fact, he was considering making himself a proper part of their family very soon. That thought made his hand slide to his left pocket instinctively. The ring box rested in it neatly. He had been planning this for a while. Today was the day.

A shadow fell over him and he looked up expectantly. Nikolina stood in the doorway. His heart leapt when he saw her and he jumped up, but she wasn't paying attention. Her gaze was still on her notes and her brow was furrowed with obvious stress.

He hesitated. Was now the right time? She was so wound up over her case that it might not go down well if he interrupted her, whatever the reason was.

While he was still considering what to do next, Ilya appeared behind Nikolina and broke the silence. "Are you two coming down for breakfast or not?" he questioned.

"We'll be right there." Antonin nodded. He reached out and

tugged the papers from Nikolina's hands, "There's time to work later, babe, let's go and eat," he encouraged.

"But..." she looked anxious, her eyes following her notes as he dumped them on the bed.

"The case will be fine," he tried to soothe her, pulling her into a hug and rubbing her back gently, "I know you don't believe me," he added, realising how empty his words sounded, "but can you at least eat something before you start worrying about work again? Otherwise, you'll scare me."

She leaned against him and allowed him to try to calm her down. He was right, it wasn't working, but she didn't want him to start worrying as well. So she sighed and gave a small nod. "Okay, fine..." she wasn't hungry, but maybe if she ate, her family and her boyfriend would all stop worrying about her.

"Great," Antonin smiled and pecked her forehead, a quick gesture of affection, "Now let's go."

Reassured now that he had got their attention, Ilya led the way as they trouped back downstairs to eat.

For Antonin, breakfast was the end of his peaceful morning full of hopeful thoughts for the future. As soon as he had eaten, Ilya announced that it was time to leave and he had dash off upstairs again to grab his bag.

On the way back out he blew a kiss to Nikolina, who was once again lost in work and barely seemed to notice. Then, he hurried to the car, eager to catch up with Ilya who was already waiting in the vehicle with the engine running.

He threw his bag into the boot and jumped into the passenger seat hastily, fastening his safety belt. "Ready to go!" he called to Ilya.

These mornings.... They were great, but they were always a rush as well. It would be stressful, but hey, at least it was livelier than his boring old commute.

As the car pulled out of the drive, Ilya struck up a casual conversation, "By the way, I have a surprise for you at work today," he revealed.

That struck Antonin as odd. Ilya usually took work very seriously. It wasn't the time or place that he would arrange a 'surprise'. Besides, he wasn't big on surprises.

"What are you up to?" Antonin questioned curiously.

"I'm not 'up to' anything. It's just that I've been thinking," Ilya started to explain himself, " it's about time you had your first assignment. Now, I think I've found a perfect case."

"You have? That's great!" Antonin couldn't hide his excitement. It wasn't that he didn't like the everyday parts of his job, but he had been longing for a little more action away from the confines of the station, for a long time.

Ilya chuckled, the younger man's reaction confirming all his suspicions. "I thought you might say that," he replied. "Let's get to the station so that I can officially fill you in," he added.

"Of course, protocol," Antonin rolled his eyes. Now he was eager for the details but would have to wait.

PREPARING

It wasn't until later at the debriefing in Ilya's office at the police station that Antonin learned the full, thrilling and slightly terrifying nature of this assignment.

"We're dealing with a complicated case here," Ilya began solemnly, hoping to get Antonin to look beyond the idea of an adventure and take this seriously, "There have been threats, disappearances and even a few deaths."

That revelation caught the younger man by surprise. Antonin had been expecting a bigger case than the usual, run-of-the-mill stuff, of course, but this wasn't something he had even considered.

"Do we have any leads at all? It's not going to be easy to sort this kind of thing out..." he mused aloud, at a loss for where to start.

Ilya nodded, "The local department have some suspicions about a mafia operation, you'll have to talk to them to find out more," he explained.

"Huh?" Antonin frowned, confused. Why would he be dealing with a different department in this case? "Is this not a local issue?" he questioned further, needing to know more.

"No, it's not. In fact, the case is in Yaroslavl. But Chief Sunnikov, a friend of mine who happens to run the department there, specifically asked for outside help. She didn't tell me why, but I assume she wants to be sure there's no conflict of interest or internal corruption." Ilya explained.

Once again, Antonin found himself feeling very confused. He was torn now as well. He had been craving a case of his own that held a little more action than the mundane daily part of his job. This definitely ticked that box, but he was a little scared. And then there was the other problem that Ilya seemed to have forgotten about...

"Well, I'm flattered that you thought of me, but Yaroslavl is 173 miles away. How exactly am I supposed to get there?" he raised the topic.

But Ilya hadn't forgotten at all, "I was just getting to the travel arrangements," he explained, "You can take a car, we've got some new ones coming in. And Chief Sunnikov says she's arranged somewhere for you to stay. When you get there, check in with her and she'll fill you in on the details."

"Right," Antonin nodded. Well, at least that cleared that up. The only remaining question now was whether this was going to be a thrilling adventure to talk about for years to come or a terrifying near-death experience.

And there was only one way to find out, so he decided to be brave. "I'd better go and get a car, then. And pack some things."

Ilya got up, "I'll get a car ready for you," he agreed.

They made their way back outside and over to the garage that sat on the other side of the car park. This was where they kept the cars that weren't being used. It was shut up at the moment, but Ilya had some keys on him and soon unlocked it, pulling open the doors.

"There we are, then, take your pick," he gestured to the rows of cars inside.

Antonin was insistently interested, stepping inside and walking around the cars as he carefully inspected them. "Hm... Well, I better go unmarked, if there's a chance I'm heading into an organised crime group's headquarters. Don't want to spook them. Or be a target," he mused, moving along the line, "That just leaves the question, which of the unmarked ones is fastest?"

Ilya rolled his eyes, "Enough of that. Pretending to be a speed demon when you haven't driven in five years."

"Hey, I've just been saving my skills for the right opportunity. Besides, I might need to make a fast getaway. Or give chase, or..." Antonin began to protest.

"You watch too many movies," His boss commented, before grabbing some keys from a nearby shelf and tossing them to him. "These are for that one," he pointed to the car Antonin was stood by, "It's pretty quick since you're looking for a new toy. And it'll get the job done as well. Just try to bring it back in one piece."

The other man caught the keys and rolled his eyes, "Yeah, yeah, sure. I better take it home and get some stuff packed," he said, opening the car door.

"Just a minute, I'll get your other stuff from my car," Ilya reminded him. He'd forgotten about his bag, which contained all his usual work stuff and left it in the other man's car.

After a few moments, he came back and handed over the bag, which Antonin bunged carelessly into the front passenger seat of his new car, before sliding into the driver's seat. "Right, time to go then. I'll let you know how it goes when it's all over," he told Ilya casually, putting a brave face on the whole situation.

Ilya nodded, "You do that. And bring yourself back in one piece, as well." he told him, which Antonin guessed was as close to a fond farewell as he was going to get.

He pulled the door shut, strapped himself in and started the engine, cursing when his first attempt stalled. His break from driving had taken more of a toll than he expected. But on his second attempt, he pulled away, waving half-dismissively and half as a goodbye to the laughing Ilya, who had found his mistake quite amusing.

Now where to? Antonin wondered as he pulled out of the police station car park. The best bet would probably be back to the Moroz family's home. While he hadn't technically moved in, he had most of his possessions in Nikolina's room at the moment.

Besides, he would have to say goodbye to her.

That thought hit harder than he had expected. He didn't think about that earlier, but he would be going away from her for a long time. Leaving her in her current, stressed mood while she waited for her case to start that afternoon...

He groaned. This wasn't going to be easy.

But it was soon a reality that he had to face up to, as before long he was pulling up outside the house again.

He left the car, pushed open the front door and wandered inside. He waved to Sasha as he passed the other man in the living room, then made his way upstairs to Nikolina's room.

She was still sitting on her bed, going through her notes when he found her. She didn't appear to have noticed his arrival, so he called out to her softly, "Lina?"

Finally, she raised her head and looked at him, "Antonin? I thought you were at work!"

"I was..." he admitted, before hastily changing the subject, not wanting to begin the conversation on his bombshell news, "How's your prep going?"

"I'm just making sure, but I seem to have all my notes ready now," she told him. But she wasn't going to be completely distracted, "Why did you come home again?" she asked.

Well, now or never. "I... I came to get my things," he finally let it out.

She wrinkled her brow, confused, "Why?"

"I've got my first assignment," he told her, starting with the good news.

She smiled, "That's good! So, we've both got our first cases now?"

"Yep, both moving up in the world, babe," he agreed as casually as he could while picking up some of his bags. Just the ones with the clothes and other essentials, he wouldn't need the rest, would he?

No, he could leave his guitar behind, and his music books. And his comics. And...

Then the penny seemed to drop, "Do you have to go away for your assignment or something?" she asked, interrupting him as he pondered what to pack.

"Yeah..." he nodded reluctantly, "The assignment is in Yaroslavl..."

"What?!" That got her to discard her papers, at last, throwing them down on the bed and getting up, "That's miles away!"

"I know, babe," he sighed, dropping his packing and turning to her, "And I'm going to miss you while I'm gone... But I have to. They've got some serious trouble over there."

Nikolina looked torn, "I am glad you're helping and taking your job so seriously... But I will really miss you too!" She ran over to hug him. After a few moments of peace as they held one another, she finally questioned, "What kind of 'trouble' though? Will you be safe?"

"It's a mafia job," he told her. Upon seeing her concerned expression, he added, "But I'm sure I'll be in my element, finally getting some action and all."

His grin at the end of that statement must have convinced her and he thanked God that it had because otherwise, she might have noticed that he hadn't actually answered her question. He wasn't sure of that himself, and he didn't want to lie to her.

"I'd better pack," he told her, moving away again reluctantly and starting to sort his things out.

It took a little while, but eventually, he had his essential belongings all sorted out and was ready to go.

Apart from one thing. The ring box, a tiny little thing, seemed to weigh heavily in his pocket, especially with Nikolina watching him forlornly as he prepared to go.

Leaving his bags on the floor, he pulled her into his arms again, kissing her. When they eventually broke apart, she sighed, "I guess it is time for you to go now, then? Is this our goodbye kiss?"

"Almost," he admitted, "But before that happens, there's something I want to give you," he reached into his pocket.

"What is it?"

Taking out the ring, he smiled at her sweetly, "It's just a promise. I want to be able to promise that, when I get back, we'll get married. Will you agree to that?" he asked as he opened the box.

She threw her arms around him again, "Of course!"

He laughed cautiously, "Lina, Lina! You're going to knock it on the floor in a minute, calm down!"

She let go and slipped the ring onto her hand instead, looking sheepish, "Sorry, I got excited. But still... This is just about the best way to say goodbye if you have to go," she told him, cheering up a little.

"I know," he grinned, before pulling her into another kiss.

That was their final goodbye though, as time was marching on, so when they parted, he gathered his bags and headed back to his car, ready to start his mission at last.

THE MISSION BEGINS

All packed up and ready, Antonin sat in the car and stared out through the windscreen. He had a long journey ahead of him, and while it might be exciting, it was beginning to dawn on him that it would be very difficult as well. Leaving his fiancée had already sobered him up after his initial excitement, and part of him suspected that was only going to be the tip of the iceberg as far as challenges were concerned.

But it was too late to turn back now. Besides, there was only one way to find out what the mission held, challenge or adventure. He started up the car and put his foot down firmly, taking off into the distance.

He kept driving, making his way through the city, then onto the open roads leading from it. He raced through villages, towns and cities of all kinds without a glance, determined to get to Yaroslavl and get the mission underway.

It took three whole hours, but soon he was driving into the city. He slowed down as he entered, taking his time to look around. Everything seemed quite normal. In fact, he had driven through several cities just like this on the way here. There were clusters of houses, shops, a port with a large river... And yet there didn't seem to be anyone about.

He frowned. It was lunchtime on a Tuesday, he would have expected to see people on their lunch breaks, milling around and chatting, heading to the restaurants or shops. There were very few people around, and they hurried from place to place, looking around suspiciously. Several glared at him as they saw him watching.

Either people in this city are *really* unfriendly, or the crime spree has had some kind of effect on the local atmosphere, he thought to himself as he drove down the main street.

But that was something he would have to investigate further after he had a little more information about what was going on around here. Time to find the local police station and find out what they knew so far.

He drove on, peering around for any sign that told him where to go. Feeling lost was bizarre to him, he was used to living and working in a city he knew like the back of his hand. But this was all new.

However, after a while of aimless, confused driving around, Antonin arrived at the police station. He pulled into the car park, stopped and jumped out. Well, here he was. The mission was beginning in earnest now.

Wandering in, he made his way to the front desk and showed his badge, explaining who he was and why he was there. That was simple enough, and before long he was shown into an office to talk with the chief.

Chief Sunnikov was a tall, stately woman with slick, tied back grey hair. She looked to be at least in her sixties, but she got up and moved to greet him with an easy kind of speed and energy that took him by surprise, shoving her files aside and stepping in front of her desk swiftly.

She took his hand and shook it heartily, "Welcome to Yaroslavl, Officer Jelennski. I *am* sorry to drag you into this, but I suspect this case won't get solved without outside help, and Chief Moroz can always be relied on to support me. Since he recommended you, I'm sure you'll be a great asset,"

He hadn't expected her to be quite so talkative and stood there, a little taken aback. Eventually, he rallied, "Thank you, Ma'am... Um, well, I'll do my best." he said, though he was a little nervous now. She seemed to have very high expectations.

"What's the situation, though? I'm afraid we didn't get many details," he got to the main point of his visit: Finding out more about his case.

"Oh, yes, I forgot! I didn't want to share too much important information by mail in case it was intercepted. Sit down, and I'll fill you in!" she nodded, heading back to her own seat with him trailing behind her.

It took a while for her to find the relevant file, jiggling her paperwork around until she located it. Then she slid it over the desk to him. "These are all the notes we have on the case, but I'll talk you through the important parts anyway..."

He sighed in relief. It may only be a surprisingly slim file, but he didn't want to get anything wrong on his first case. Listening to her clear tones made him feel more confident that trying to decipher her handwriting did. A glance just showed squiggles. Lost, he sat back and let her take over.

"To start with, as I made clear in my earlier notes, there have been several incidents, most of them violent and all of them quite horrible. They all appear to be linked to one house," she began her explanation, reaching forward and tapping the first page of the file.

The piece of paper had an address printed on it, above a few images of the house. It was an odd place. The building was large, towering above those on the other side of it. It was made of dark stone and had a black door set in its centre. Dotted around were little windows, covered by black curtains.

None of this was particularly odd in itself, despite a rather dull colour scheme, but the images gave him a sense of foreboding.

"This is the place? Any idea what's going on there?" he asked.

She nodded, "We suspect that the family who live there are running some kind of mafia business," she reiterated the suspicion Ilya had mentioned, "These people, the Volkov family, they have a reputation among the locals, but we can't get anything solid. People are too scared. They're definitely a strange bunch though. There are loads of them living there and they all keep to themselves."

Antonin considered this. It didn't look hopeful. If no one was coming forward with solid evidence and the family avoided all interaction, how could they get to know the secrets behind the family's activities?

"Do you have any leads at all?" he questioned hopefully.

"There's one," the Chief revealed, "I think the ringleader is Vladimir Volkov. His daughter, Dariya, doesn't appear to like him very much. And she seems to the weak link in their operations too. I've been wondering if she's an unwilling part of all this, but nothing's come of it yet. Try chasing it up. If she isn't on board with Vladimir's plans, there's a chance that she'll help us out. But it won't be easy to persuade her. We can't just storm in and demand she talks to us."

"So, what *do* we do?" Antonin pressed, sensing that she had some kind of plan.

"I think the best way to handle this is to have an undercover operative get close to her, then see what she knows," Sunnikov explained, "That's what I want you to do. That's why I asked for outside help. Someone from our force would be recognised."

Antonin nodded. That made sense, but there was one thing bothering him, "How do I get close to her if they all keep to themselves?"

"Dariya is the only one who tends to go out. Occasionally, she goes to the Blue Mango Club, in the city centre. Go there this evening and look for her." she pulled out a picture of Dariya, "If you see her, try to get her attention. If you have to, seduce her," the Chief instructed.

"Right. The Club. Got it." Antonin nodded awkwardly, choosing to ignore the 'seduce her' comment for now. He wasn't going there!

"Anything else, Ma'am?" he asked.

She nodded, "Two things," she handed him another piece of paper, "Here are the directions to your hotel. The expenses have been paid, so don't worry about that."

"Thanks. What else was there?"

"You might want to change in the men's room before you go. You're supposed to be undercover from now on and walking around in full uniform will probably attract attention," she pointed out.

"Right..." That might explain the odd looks he had got earlier. He bid her goodbye on that note, wanting to change and get on with his case as soon as possible.

She watched him walk away, then tidied up her abandoned paperwork and crossed to the window, glancing out across the car park and into her city. All she could do now was hope for the best.

He ran back to the car, grabbing his bag full of clothes and tossing the papers into the boot in its place. He was rushing now, eager to get on with his case, and severely startled a maintenance man who was painting new lines on the parking bays.

The man jumped up, splashing paint on his car and shouting, but Antonin didn't have time for him, his mind full of his case, "Sorry!" He yelled over his shoulder as he tore off into the station again.

He got a nod in return, but was already back inside, oblivious to it as he made his way down the corridors. It was only then that he slowed down a little, in order to follow the Chief's advice. He didn't want to put his life on the line by blowing his cover before the mission even began. So, he slipped into the men's room to change. Once he was suitably dressed in a more casual outfit of jeans and a blue t-shirt, he checked himself in the mirror.

The surprises of the day had already taken a toll on him. Though he was normally pale, he looked even more so now, and there were bags under his indigo-blue eyes.

Well, he hadn't slept properly for a couple of days, he had been considering his future too much. It wasn't all to do with the mission, though he suspected that wouldn't help at all.

He ran his fingers through his chestnut-brown hair, following it down until the waves fell around his neck, and sighed. Tiredness and stress were just what he needed on a mission where things might get physical.

Still, he supposed, despite his health, he was in pretty good shape. Standing at 6'2, he was a pretty big guy, with muscles to back him up.

He just hoped he wasn't going to need them. But that was something he would only find out later. Right now, he had to go and check into the hotel. Maybe then he could try and get a little rest before he went to try to find this 'Dariya' girl.

DARIYA

The club was dark and full of noise. It was very disorientating to Antonin as he stumbled inside. This wasn't his kind of thing and never had been, so he felt lost.

Once he adjusted to the light level, he tried to shut out the thumping music and the shouts of the more intoxicated revellers while he looked for his target.

He glanced down at the picture Chief Sunnikov had given him. He was looking for a young woman with tan-coloured skin, shoulder-length black curls and piercing grey eyes. She had a distinctive scar along her left cheekbone as well, which he hoped would make her easier to spot.

Committing this information to memory, he slipped the picture into his pocket and scanned the room instead.

The first time he looked, his eyes passed right over her and he didn't even notice. It was only on his second, puzzled look around the room that he noticed her. The girl was slouching against the wall in a corner. She didn't look like she was there to party like everyone else was. For one thing, she was dressed in a plain black, oversized tracksuit. And she blended into her shadowy little corner easily.

She was just standing there, watching everyone else carefully.

Well, at least he had found her. He supposed that was progress. But now he had a harder task ahead of him: getting close to her without arousing any kind of suspicion.

He made his way over to her as casually as he could, even though he felt out of place here. "Hi..." he tried to start a conversation.

She looked up at him with an expression of genuine confusion, as if she couldn't quite work out what he was.

He didn't realise he seemed *that* out of place, but apparently, he did. Perhaps he wasn't very good at this undercover business. He was just pondering this and trying to decide whether or not he was going to get a response when she spoke.

"Do you want something?" she asked. The comment wasn't as abrupt as he had expected it to be. She sounded quite polite, just at a loss for any reason why he was here, talking to her.

Why *was* he here? He thought hard for some sort of excuse and blushed when the only words that came to him were Sunnikov's embarrassing comments from earlier.

No, he reminded himself. That's not happening. Maybe just... Try to be her friend?

"I just wondered if you'd like to hang out for a bit," he asked her, again with a degree of forced casualness.

She gave him a doubting look, "Really? That's all?"

"Yeah," he nodded.

For a moment, he thought it would really be that easy, that they would simply become friends and that that would give him inside access to all the Volkov family's hidden little secrets. Because for a split second, there was a flicker of something like hope in her eyes.

Then it was gone, and she shook her head with a snort of disbelief, "Yeah right! What are you really here for?"

Now she had him backed into a corner and he didn't know how to persuade her now. He sighed. He seemed to be all out of options, so he took a deep breath and went for it.

"I just thought I'd buy the prettiest girl here a nice drink," he told her, trying to sound sincere, though talking in even a vaguely flirtatious manner to someone other than his girlfriend felt weird and awkward.

But Dariya nodded as though he had passed some kind of test or at least done what she had expected of him. "Alright then, go for it. I'll have a margarita," she told him.

"And I'll have your phone number," he replied, trying to at least get something useful out of this interaction since it had been a dead-end so far. But as soon as he turned up the flirting a bit, he felt sick. That was a stupid thing to say!

She laughed, "Forward, aren't you? Alright, if that's how you want to play it, you get my number when I get my drink," she retorted.

He rolled his eyes as he walked away to the bar. This girl seemed pretty demanding. He hadn't even got a 'thank you' yet. Then again, her attitude and her tone of voice didn't seem to match up. It was the same with her dismissal of him at first. She hadn't been rude, despite her sharp words. She seemed calm, even when what she was saying wasn't. It was almost like listening to a bad actor read from a script, speaking the words without their real emotions.

Perhaps that was it. It occurred to him that there might be more to Dariya Volkova than there seemed to be. He certainly hoped so, anyway, since she was supposed to be their lead and it didn't seem like she was helping him bust a crime ring right now.

Nevertheless, he grabbed her drink and made his way back over to her. She took the drink, "Thanks," she said finally, sipping it.

"No problem," he nodded, then thought for something to say. It was difficult. He wanted to blurt out questions about her family, but had to act normally instead, "So, what's your name?" he asked her.

She raised an eyebrow, looking surprised by his question, and a little disbelieving. "You're not from round here, are you?" she asked after a few moments.

"No," he shook his head. "Why, are you famous or something?"

"You could say that," she nodded, "My family practically runs this city."

Bingo, he grinned to himself. Finally, he was getting somewhere, "Oh, how's that? Is your father the mayor or something?"

"Something," she responded with a smile that didn't reach her eyes. For a second, he felt nervous, as though her mismatching words and tones, expressions and feelings, were all some kind of warning that he should turn and run.

Perhaps she sensed his unease, because she stopped for a second, then gave him a more relaxed, genuine smile. "It's actually refreshing to meet someone who *doesn't* know me. I'm Dariya, nice to meet you," she greeted him.

He smiled, "It's nice to meet you too. I'm Antonin. I'm just here from Moscow on a business trip, so yeah, I don't know a lot about how things work around here," he told her as much of the truth as he could without giving himself away.

"Would you like to?" she asked suddenly, and again, it was jarring.

So jarring that it threw him, and he had to question her, "Would I like to what?"

"Would you like to learn how things work here? I can teach you, so you feel a little more comfortable while you're here. It must be very different, after all."

"Uh... Sure," he gave a confused nod. It was a strange offer, but it helped his goal of getting more information, after all.

Dariya smiled in that odd, grating way again, "Great! You should come and meet my family!"

"Now who's forward?" he responded before he could help himself, a little stunned by the suddenness of that invitation, though theoretically, it was what he had wanted.

"That's not what I meant, silly! I just meant that if you want to know how things work in Yaroslavl, you need to meet them," she explained herself.

More information. So, the Volkov family really were the key to all this. That meant, despite how odd Dariya's offer was and the fact that he felt as though it'd be walking into a trap, he really ought to go and get to know them.

"Alright then. When?" he asked.

He wasn't expecting her to down the rest of her drink and say, "Now," Before striding off towards the exit, leaving him running along behind her to try and keep up.

As he dashed through the crowded club, he could only wonder what to expect from meeting her notorious family so suddenly.

THE VOLKOVS

The walk was surprisingly short, and soon Dariya stopped outside the house. Antonin glanced up at it. It was the same as it had been in the picture, but somehow more real now that it was towering over him. He wasn't sure he wanted to go inside.

It was a little late to make that decision, "Here we are!" Dariya turned to him with that same bright, false smile.

He wondered if he should call her out or question her about it, ask if she was okay. This didn't seem normal. But they barely knew each other, she wouldn't open up to him, would she?

Besides, she was already shoving the door open. He reluctantly trailed after her, stepping inside.

The house was even weirder on the inside because suddenly, everything was different. It had been big, dark and looming outside. Yet now, he had stepped into a narrow, white-washed, corridor.

He blinked and looked around. This place was definitely weird, but he couldn't exactly put his finger on why it felt that way. So, he kept following Dariya, hoping she would lead him to some kind of answer.

She led him down the corridor and opened a small door at the end, which brought them out in a much larger, but equally featureless, white room. This one was crowded, and Antonin couldn't help but stare as he took it all in.

There seemed to be loads of them, milling all around the room, chattering incessantly. But they all looked the same. Not just vaguely related, but almost identical to one another, down to small details like the scar they all bore on their left cheeks.

The effect was quite disconcerting. It was also very strange and made him curious as to exactly what was going on here, why they all looked like that and how the scar had come to mark them all like that.

There were so many questions, but he couldn't ask any of them in case they aroused their suspicions. So, he simply stood silently behind Dariya and waited to see what would happen next.

Dariya cleared her throat and her various relatives turned to look at her curiously.

She gave them a cheerful wave, "Hey! I just thought I'd bring my new boyfriend to meet you all!" she trilled with a bright smile.

Antonin stared at her, "Boyfriend?! We jus-- Ouch!!"

He had been hissing a rebuke at her under his breath, feeling horrible at being called some random woman's boyfriend when he had a bride-to-be waiting for him at home, but Dariya's movements were swift, and her elbow was surprisingly sharp.

He fell silent, his ribs aching and wondered why she had suddenly attacked. They had seemed to be getting along... Perhaps she hadn't wanted him to speak up and make a scene in front of her family, but he hadn't meant to, which was why he had whispered to her.

Perhaps it was best just to keep quiet and see what the Volkov family had in store for him.

They were watching him quite closely now and he shifted from foot to foot, feeling uncomfortable under the pressure of their staring eyes.

"Another one?" Someone spoke up at last. The voice was sharp and sarcastic. It seemed to be enjoying a rather nasty joke at their expense, "Where did you find this one?" The questions were addressed to Dariya. Everyone stared at Antonin, but no one spoke to him.

They crowded around though, others joining in and asking more questions about him. They were basic questions - His name, where he came from, how they met - But the scenario and their attitudes turned it into some kind of strange interrogation.

Dariya handled it well though, introducing him and talking quite calmly about their first meeting - Though she carefully made it sound as though it was more than five minutes ago. She seemed quite used to handling her family. And, he noticed as she elaborated about their 'relationship', quite good at lying to them.

He wondered why that was. Perhaps she was keeping secrets and therefore, really was the key to finding out all about the local crime spree. Or perhaps she lied to help their illegal enterprises. It didn't seem like she was helping them now, but she was very good at lying, perhaps she was deceiving him too.

Watching the conversation reminded him that he had to be on his toes about that kind of thing anyway and that he mustn't fall into the trap of trusting anyone here.

But it also made him surer than ever that he needed Dariya's help. There was definitely something very odd about this place and this family, and they were never going to co-operate with an outsider since they completely ignored him.

He couldn't trust her. But he couldn't do this without her.

He just wished he knew what she was up to. She must have brought him here for a reason, but now she was spinning strange stories to her ever-stranger family members while he stood, quiet and ignored, trying to observe and failing.

He couldn't understand any of what was going on here. Even their conversations were beyond him, despite the fact that they spoke perfectly normally and seemed to be talking about him. But the conversations were full of lies and little inflexions that made him question what was being said. Perhaps they had slipped some form of code into their conversation to confuse him or talk about him to his face and get away with it.

It was the kind of conversation that seemed perfectly innocent but made him feel awkward and overly aware of every little comment. He hadn't encountered that since high school, but they were much better at it and much more persistent.

It was starting to make him want to scream.

Very softly, a door shut behind him.

No one had heard it open, nor had they heard the front door. But as it shut, the conversation came to an abrupt halt.

Antonin followed the others as their gazes turned. He needed to know what had caused such a sudden change in them.

There was a man standing in the doorway. He was tall and well-built, his tan skin mostly covered by his dark suit. He had a prominent scar on his cheek, and jet-black hair that was flecked with grey, with a beard to match.

His eyes were lighter grey than those of the others. They were so pale that he almost looked as though he had blind, milky eyes. But he could see. The look on his face suggested he could see through souls.

Antonin recognised him instantly, from the pictures in the file. It was Vladimir Volkov.

The silence was finally broken as he stepped forward with a benevolent smile, "I'm home, children. Who's our guest?" he added, his gaze wandering to Antonin.

It felt as though he was looking through him, but his grey eyes had settled on his face. They were slightly defocused, gazing left in a dreamy kind of way.

That was easily more uncomfortable than the hard stares and gossipy whispers that Antonin had been longing to escape from. Perhaps he should have been careful what he wished for.

Again, Dariya filled the breach quite calmly, "This is Antonin, my new boyfriend," she explained, "Antonin, this is my father," she added, introducing them properly.

Damn, Antonin thought to himself. He'd been hoping that Vladimir would be as rude as most of his relatives and ignore him, so he could get away without having to talk to the creepy older man.

Instead, he rather reluctantly shook Vladimir's outstretched hand and forced a smile. "Nice to meet you," he lied.

"Yes, isn't it?" Vladimir answered cryptically, holding onto his hand for a little too long. "Why did my lovely little Dariya decide to bring you here today? Are you planning to join our family sometime soon?" he asked him, still looking right through him.

Turning red, Antonin looked desperately to Dariya for help. She didn't look much more comfortable than he was with her father's sudden, blunt questions, but she rallied, "We... We haven't had that conversation yet, Papa," she told him as carefully and tactfully as she could.

Vladimir looked genuinely stunned by that news, then, after a few moments of consideration, politely asked, "Would you like to? We can leave you two alone for a private chat if you want."

The two looked at one another a little helplessly. This was getting worse by the second. Then Antonin sighed. The only way he could think of to make this experience less uncomfortable was to ask Dariya some questions he couldn't ask in front of everyone.

"Uh... Yes, I think that might be a good idea," he said finally, needing to get some answers whether it blew his cover or not. Or at least to get five minutes away from the strange, staring Volkovs.

PLANNING

The door closed, leaving Antonin and Dariya alone. He waited for the footsteps of the other Volkovs to fade away before he turned to her and demanded to know, "Alright, *what the hell is going on?*"

Perhaps for someone supposed to be undercover, this question lacked a certain amount of tact, but he was at a loss for any other words to express his current feelings.

Dariya paused. She walked to the door and rested her head against it for a moment. Then she ran her hands over her clothes, smoothing them out. Something fell to the floor. She trod on it.

All this out of the way, she finally began to speak, "Okay, okay, I owe you an explanation," she admitted. Now, her voice was different. The edge of cheer that made her seem as though she knew what she was doing was gone. She sounded nervous.

"Yeah, that would be great. I mean, things are strange enough here, without one drink being enough to make us boyfriend and girlfriend and that somehow giving your family a right to talk over my head!" he retorted, genuinely bewildered by everything that had just happened.

Dariya sighed, "Look, I didn't want to put you in an awkward situation, but ultimately, I had a choice to make. And I admit I made the selfish choice. But I needed your help."

That wasn't what he had expected her to say. Why would she need some random stranger's help, assuming he hadn't already managed to blow his cover? He didn't know how to respond to that, especially not without any context, so he waited patiently for her to explain herself.

Eventually, after glancing at the silent young man nervously, she started again:

"You see, my family are... Abnormal. I'm sure you've noticed that. But they're worse than that. My father only runs this place because everyone here's scared to death of him, myself included. He's a monster, and he wants to make the rest of us monsters. As I said, no one here's ever going to oppose him or live long enough to do so effectively. So, I wait for a stranger to come here, let them know that it's not a good place to be, and try to convince them to get me away from here. That's why I 'date' a lot of people, 'cause my father only lets me bring people who might 'join the family' here. But you don't want to be a part of this family!"

She began to ramble now, her voice wavering as her distress became more and more apparent. She had hidden it well beneath her brittle smile, but now she was on the verge of tears.

And, to Antonin's horror, he felt like celebrating this announcement, because it meant their intelligence was right. Perhaps if he told her the truth, she would help him. Then, at the back of his mind, the tiny voice of doubt spoke up. Should he reveal his cover so soon? He didn't know that he could trust her... Though her emotion *did* seem genuine.

But if this was some kind of ploy, if they already knew he was here to take them down, then the stakes could be pretty high. They might trap him or kill him.

"Well, will you help me?" Dariya's pleading tones cut through his thoughts.

His brain whispered that he should proceed with caution, but his heart couldn't ignore her distress.

"I'll try to," he offered a compromise, not telling her the truth immediately, but offering help anyway. "But..." he hesitated again.

Should he tell her? If he was going to help her, he would have to, sooner or later, right? After all, she wanted him to take her away from the city, but he couldn't just yet, because of his job.

He ran the issue through his mind again, then began again. "I'll help, but I have something to explain to you first," he revealed.

She nodded, "I'll listen if it'll get me out of here."

"It will. You see, that's kind of why I'm here in the first place. I'm a police officer," he confessed, "I want to stop your father, but I need your help getting some evidence against him."

"I know. Why did you think I asked you?" She replied calmly.

He stared. Seriously? His first ever undercover mission and he had been figured out by some random woman?

"For real?!" He wished he could have thought of a better response, but shock got the better of him.

She nodded. "You spend enough time in this dump and you soon figure out when someone doesn't fit in. So, I take it you are here to help?"

At least that explained why she had gone from treating him as a weirdo to being his new 'girlfriend', he supposed.

Nodding, he explained, "I came to find you on purpose, hoping I could infiltrate your family and find out what's been going on here. We've known it's not right for a while..."

"You can say that again... It's actually a relief to tell someone how I really feel about them for once, instead of playing along," she said with a sigh.

Antonin nodded, relieved to start getting things off his chest, now that he was over the shock of his swift discovery, "It's definitely nice to drop all the acting. All that flirting and pretending to date was... Weird," he commented.

Dariya pouted, "I'm not that bad, am I?" she asked.

Despite their more serious conversation earlier, he couldn't help but chuckle at her expression. "No, no, that's not what I meant. I'm just not used to undercover work yet," he tried to explain.

She sighed, "When I figured out you were a police officer, I kind of hoped for someone with experience, not a rookie..."

Now it was his turn to be hurt, "I'm not a rookie! I've dealt with lots of cases, I'm just used to being able to operate with others, not hide away. And I certainly didn't plan to have to cheat on my fiancée for this job!" His words were full of her anger, and her surprise was evident in her expression.

"I'm sorry, I didn't know that! I guess this is a very unusual case..." she admitted, before smiling, "It's cute that you're so worried about your fiancée, but we're only pretending," she tried to reassure him.

He calmed down a little. It was just the stress, the stress of working so hard, under these unusual conditions, and away from his beloved Nikolina.

"I'm sorry too, I'm just not used to pretending, undercover work is hard..." he sighed.

"Well, I guess so, since I caught you," She joked, before taking on a more serious tone, "But then, I'm barely used to not pretending to be something I'm not around here," she told him sympathetically.

"But if we have to get on with a case to stop Papa, then I'll do everything I can to help you out! In fact, I think I know where to start. We'll just have to plan it out carefully so that we don't get caught. If my father finds out, he'll try to kill you," she revealed, changing the subject suddenly.

"Yeah, we'll definitely need to think about how to avoid that at some point," Antonin agreed, repressing a shiver. He didn't want her to see that he was scared, but Vladimir was definitely disconcerting.

He tried to focus on the positives, telling her, "I'm glad you've got an idea, I hope it'll work. So long as we can prove Vladimir's committing crimes here, we can finally lock him up."

Doubt clouded her features briefly, "And I won't get into any trouble?"

"Not if you help me," he assured her.

"Great!" she smiled, and it was finally a genuine smile. "Then we can get to wo..." she paused partway through her sentence and shushed him suddenly, whispering, "They're coming back!"

Instantly, they both fell into silence and straightened up, doing their best to look innocent. A moment later, Vladimir opened the door and the family crowded back into the room, still staring at the 'couple'.

"Well?" Vladimir asked, "Have you come to a decision yet?"

They exchanged glances awkwardly. What was it they had been supposed to discuss again? In the heat of the moment, it had all slipped their minds.

Dariya remembered first and hastily jumped to come up with an excuse, "Not exactly, no! We thought it might be better if

Antonin moved in for a bit, so we can all get to know one another better and bond as a family before he," she paused, turning slightly red, "...You know..." her voice faded to a mumble.

Despite that part, Antonin had to applaud her. She must have been dealing with her father's questioning for a long time to be this good at coming up with rapid-fire lies. He wasn't entirely sure that was a good thing, though. He had been raised to believe any kind of lie was wrong, hence all this undercover work didn't sit well for him. But he understood there was a need here. For Dariya, it must be a kind of survival instinct. And for him... Well, it would have to become one.

He tried to think of something comforting, and Nikolina came to mind. She always said that sometimes, lies were necessary. He hadn't believed her until now. Perhaps he never should have doubted her. When he got home, he'd tell her how right she was, while he held her in his arms.

"Antonin?!" Dariya's voice nudged at him and he looked around guiltily, embarrassed to be here, pretending to be her boyfriend, while he dreamed of another woman.

"Uhh... Yeah?" he questioned.

"I said, when do you want to move in?" she asked him.

'Never' was his first thought. He didn't want to live with these frankly creepy people. But he had to think of his mission, and the sooner they could start to gather evidence, the better.

So, he said, "Can we start moving in tomorrow morning?"

Vladimir chuckled, "You're keen, aren't you? Alright, you can share Dariya's room. I'm sure she'll help you move in tomorrow. Then later in the week, once you've settled in, we can properly welcome you to the family..." he smiled welcomingly.

Antonin didn't fully understand that comment, but it made him want to run as far away as possible. Instead, he nodded mutely and glanced at Dariya nervously, hoping her plan was something special so they could get this over with as quickly as possible.

THE FIRST SECRET

The next day, Antonin woke up with a crick in his neck and groaned, sitting up.

"I told you you should have taken the bed," Dariya told him, looking down at him with a concerned frown.

"It's fine," he shrugged, instantly regretting the movement.

Sleeping on her bedroom floor wasn't the best idea he had ever had, but Vladimir had been quite insistent that he stay the night, but then hadn't given him his own room. Since he was pretending to be Dariya's boyfriend, he had been assumed that he would stay with her. And, of course, her room only had the one bed. He had felt it too mean to kick the young woman he was supposed to be helping out of her own bed, even if she had offered, so he had settled for the floor.

Unfortunately, it didn't seem as though this house was designed for comfort, even in the bedrooms. Dariya's room was as plain, empty and featureless as the rest of the house. There wasn't even a carpet to cushion him, only the wooden floor. He had managed a few hours of sleep, but it was still barely getting light, and he knew he wouldn't get back to sleep now.

That left him at a loss for what to do now. It seemed early to get up - Especially in a house that wasn't his - and risk disturbing other people.

Speaking of which... He looked over at Dariya, "How come you're awake? Did I disturb you?" he asked.

She shook her head, "Nah, I don't usually sleep very well anyway."

An idea occurred to him, "Anyone else likely to be up? Maybe we can look around for some evidence..."

She thought about this for a moment, "I don't think so. The guards don't start work until later in the day, I'm pretty sure, and Papa isn't an early riser..." she explained, thinking aloud as she went through the routines of anyone who might get in the way. "We should get away with it," she nodded, "C'mon!"

After her realisation, she wasted no time at all. Jumping out of bed in her nightgown, she didn't even get dressed before she ran off. It was all Antonin could do to get up and follow her.

She hurried past rows of doors and downstairs. They ran back through the living room where Antonin had first encountered the other Volkovs, and through some more similar rooms.

Eventually, Dariya reached a door and fiddled with it. "Damn, it's locked. Hang on, I know he hides the key around here somewhere..." she muttered, looking around.

A few minutes later, she discovered the key embedded in a candlestick. It was a decent hiding place, but Vladimir could have done with decorating a bit more if he wanted it to be convincing, Antonin couldn't help thinking. In a house this bare, anything unnecessary like a candle stood out. But that didn't matter, and he was probably overthinking, slipping into work-mode and looking for clues already. He tried to ignore that instinct and followed Dariya as she unlocked the door and slipped into a corridor.

It was much darker in this part of the house, which lacked any windows to let in natural light. He was beginning to wonder if the candle was unnecessary after all when Dariya finally found the light switch and flicked it on. They were in a long corridor that had a steep flight of steps at the other end. Dariya led the way determinedly, and he followed her, a little nervous.

"What exactly are we going to find down here?" he asked.

"My father's workshop," she told him.

He was still none the wiser, "Workshop? What does he do?" he questioned.

The girl sighed, "All kinds of... Unnatural things..."

"Unnatural?" Every explanation only raised more questions.

"It's... Hard to explain. Just wait, okay?" Dariya answered, clearly not wanting to continue this conversation.

Antonin still wanted to know what he was walking into, but she seemed very uncomfortable with his line of questioning, so he let it go for the moment and continued down the corridor.

They reached the steps and descended. The staircase was longer than he expected, but eventually, they reached the bottom and it opened out into a large cavern under the house.

But, unlike the house above them, this was far from empty. He stared around him, shocked and confused by what he was seeing.

"I told you," Dariya said, "He does unnatural things. Calls himself a scientist, but most of what he does here is scheming. He pays or bullies real inventors into doing the important stuff," she commented, pulling a disgusted face.

"And... That's what all this is? *Inventions?* What *for?*" He demanded to know as he gawped, turning this way and that to get a better look.

The room, if it could be called that, was huge, and it was bursting. Everywhere he looked there were tables strewn with odd bits of metal and strange devices. Some were clearly weapons, gun-shaped but lit-up like Christmas trees, suggesting they were far from ordinary weapons. Others were unrecognisable.

Some were too big for the tables and were piled up around them, in parts or completed. In the middle of the room was a sheet-draped structure that stood taller than a grown man and hummed ominously.

Dariya shrugged, "For power, I suppose. He's crazy. Thinks he's some kind of genius and that 'his' inventions will help him take control of the world," she revealed.

"And this city is his first step..." Antonin breathed. Suddenly, the puzzle pieces fell into place. This wasn't just some crime ring, run for profit. This was... Practice. See if you can scare a city into doing what you want, then a country, then the world...

He shuddered. He had to stop this. But how exactly? There was a nasty little flaw in the idea of using this for evidence.

"But I'm not sure he's technically doing anything illegal..." he frowned, confused.

These things were bizarre, of course, and definitely wrong. But were they against the law? How could they be, if the law didn't know what the hell they were?

But Dariya shook her head grimly, "Just wait," she told him, "This is just the tip of the iceberg... He's got things hidden away down here that are *definitely* illegal."

"Right. We'd better look at them, then," Antonin nodded, trying to brace himself for... Well, more than he had been previously prepared for.

It's one thing going prepared for murder, but if you suddenly find out you're dealing with world domination plans, you have to adjust. Any mind is capable of killing if pushed too far, but the kind of mind capable of planning world domination is... Special. You have to be prepared for *anything* at that point.

Dariya hesitated, her eyes fixed on the... Thing in the middle of the room. "We should, but... First, I suppose I should be completely honest with you from the start," she began.

Antonin paused, looking over at her with sudden apprehension. What was this about? The kind of conversation that started like that was never good. Had she tricked him after all, lured him down here to betray him? But if she meant to harm him, why would she reveal all this first?

Unless, of course, she didn't think he would escape. His eyes swivelled to the stairs. They weren't far away; he could run to them. But they were steep, and it was a long way up.

He shifted his weight, ready to make a break for it, just in case, then nodded, "Alright, something's up. Hit me with it."

DARIYA'S SECRET

Dariya walked across the room and yanked the sheet aside, revealing a large, almost rectangular machine. It had a glass door, shut at the moment, that closed over a human-shaped compartment. Several tubes connected to it, all leading to the compartment.

She turned back to Antonin, shaking slightly. "Do you know what this is?" she asked him.

His mind raced, but he couldn't think of an answer, so he shook his head.

"This is what brought me to life," she told him.

"Huh??" he wrinkled his brow, too confused to articulate a better response, but nevertheless needing some kind of explanation. What was she trying to say? It didn't make any sense...

Dariya sighed, seeing his confusion, "Sorry, I get that this is weird, but what I'm trying to tell you is that this," she gestured to the machine, "Is a cloning device. My father made it so that he could create... I don't know, pawns in his game. People to further his nasty little plans." she planned a face, shuddering.

Antonin surfaced slowly from his shock to try to make some sense of this, "And he... Made you with this to achieve that?"

"Not just me, but all of us. The others are all my siblings, but I was the first, his test subject. He took his own DNA, and... Altered enough for me to be a different person. My gender and things like that. But not too much, because clearly, he thinks he's the best blueprint for the rest of us," she rolled her eyes at that point.

"That sounds insane, but I have to admit it makes some sense. I did wonder how you could all look so exactly alike. Even family don't share everything..."

"Ha!" Dariya's laugh was bitter and hard now, "That's not even the tip of his insanity-iceberg! We all look *exactly* the same, right?" she raised her fingers to touch the scar on her cheek, "This isn't genetic, this is another wonderful little idea of his. It's part of a loyalty test in our 'family training'."

He stared at her, feeling sickened by the implication, "He did that to you...?"

"Worse, he made us do it to ourselves." she told him chillingly. "Still, it's better than his latest plan." she shuddered.

He flinched at the look on her face. "I hardly dare ask, but what is his latest plan?"

"He wants another generation of our family, this time from slightly different DNA, that he can raise to be even more powerful. They'll be the test subjects for his first push outside of Yaroslavl. If anything goes wrong, these children will take the fall, and if not, he uses them to take over the world..." she saw his look of horror and matched it with her own disgusted look, "But what I hate most about his plan is that he chose me. He wants me to be their template, their 'mother'. Siblings call it an honour. Perhaps it would be. I've always wanted children, but I don't want them to be weapons in this twisted game..."

The pain of what she was revealing cut her off, her voice shaking. She couldn't go on this way.

For the first time since they had met, Antonin began to feel some understanding towards Dariya. At first, she had just seemed like a closed-in girl, suppressing or faking her emotions. Then she had been... Odd, attaching herself to him too fast and lying to her family about their relationship. Then she had become an ally.

Well, more like a tool. He had to admit he had just been using her to do his job.

But now he understood that her own father, a man who should have been there to help her, had messed her up inside. She lied to survive, hid her emotions to keep him from knowing the truth and she didn't really have a life of her own.

It was a lot for someone to go through at such a young age. He knew from her file she was only twenty-two, six years younger than he was. At her age, he had just been starting his own life and had been full of excitement. She had never felt that.

And that was just the beginning. Vladimir wasn't just destroying her life. He was using her to destroy other lives. Other lives that he had created just for that reason...

That was sick. But it wasn't just morally sick, it was more personal. He didn't just want to help Dariya so that she would help him in return. He wanted her to be able to live a normal life.

And for that to be possible, he had to take Vladimir down. Not just because of the law and his job, but because this madness had to be stopped.

The sooner, the better.

"Let's get to the evidence now!" he urged her on.

She looked at him with a strange mix of confusion, hurt and anger, "Is that all you care about? Aren't you *listening?!*"

That unexpected attack stung, and he hastened to reassure her, "That's not what I meant! Look, I'm sorry if it seemed like that... It's just... He's been messing with you long enough. I want to stop him as soon as possible. Obviously, I wanted that anyway, but I didn't know how far this went. As if killing people wasn't messed up enough, he's living their lives for them too!" he let out all his disgust at what she had told him in one rant.

As he spoke, he saw Dariya's scowl fade into a smile, "Ah, there it is, the sign that you actually care. I wasn't sure you would, you know, because my father... He always says the police would never care about people like us. That all they want is to lock us away, and we shouldn't trust them. But you didn't seem like that, so I took a chance... I've never told anyone before, you see... I guess that's why I'm so defensive. Sorry," she looked a little sheepish.

"Look, some people might just want to lock you up, but that's not why I'm here. I want to help. Anyway, your father's the real criminal here, so I'll focus on him. He's probably the one you shouldn't trust," he pointed out, "But I get being defensive. It is a pretty big secret. That's why I didn't really know how to respond. But whatever you are, however, you came into being, it doesn't change that you're still you, your mind's still your own... That fact you're helping me proves that." he told her sincerely, reassured now that she had told him this. It helped him feel that he could trust her. Otherwise, she wouldn't be saying this.

Her response was a surprise though. She threw her arms around him. "Thank you!" her words came out as a cry.

A few moments later, she pulled away, blushing. "That was weird, I'm sorry. I just haven't really been accepted as anything but an extension of my father before," she told him gratefully.

"Not your fault," he shrugged it off, "Sometimes, you feel more connected to other people than your real family." he mused, thinking of his life with the Moroz family over his own, distant parents. But that was different. Both families at least treated him as a human being.

Dariya nodded, "Strangers are more like family than *him*," she didn't need to explain who *he* was.

"Not really surprising," Antonin shrugged, "After everything.

He's got a nice little benevolent act though."

"Yeah, he's well-practised," she commented disdainfully. "After he took over, he made himself mayor. That's just his public relations act... But anyway, we should probably start looking for our evidence before he gets up. I don't particularly want to be here when he decides he wants to see me."

EVIDENCE

As they had lost some time to Dariya's confession, the search for evidence became more urgent. It wouldn't be too long before Vladimir got up, and he might decide to check on his 'workshop'.

So Dariya led the way through the chamber of inventions and to another door, almost hidden as it blended in with the wall. "This is... You might want to brace yourself." she murmured nervously.

That, along with the disgusting smell that had become noticeable as he walked over to the door, was all the clues Antonin needed.

"He... He actually kept his victims' bodies down here?" he choked out over the smell. He had expected murder, he just hadn't expected the killer to be this dumb.

"He wanted to use them for experiments. He's started some... It's pretty horrible," Dariya admitted.

Antonin sighed, "Well, I guess I have to look anyway..."

Dariya nodded and covered her mouth and nose, trying to block out the rotten stench before she pulled open the door.

Antonin pulled his shirt over his face a little, hoping it would block the smell enough for his eyes to stop watering while he examined the evidence in front of him. There was a pile of bodies. More than he had been expecting. More than there had been disappearances here... They must have missed several of the cases.

The victims were all kinds of people. Their genders, races and ages didn't appear to enter into it. No, Vladimir Volkov didn't target any one group, he simply went after anyone who was in his way. And kept their bodies, in various decaying states, piled up in his basement. There was even a knife still sticking out of one of the bodies.

How could this self-proclaimed genius have covered his tracks so badly? Was it sheer stupidity, or the arrogant belief that he would never be caught?

Which led him to another question... How had it been so hard for the local police to solve this case with glaring evidence like this? When he heard that they had struggled so much, he had assumed that there was little evidence, or it would be difficult to locate. But it was just sat here, staring him in the face.

There was no way any self-respecting, genuine police officer would have missed this. There must be something bigger going on. He made a mental note to talk to Chief Sunnikov when he got out of here. She would surely investigate her department for corrupt officers...

But what if Volkov's spy or spies acted faster than he possibly could? He might be okay, she might not have told anyone about his undercover mission, but she had other key information on record, such as her suspicion of Dariya...

His new friend could be in grave danger already.

That just meant he had to work faster! He had to document this and return to the station right now so that they had the evidence to storm the place en-masse and arrest Vladimir. Confronting him alone would be stupid, but a raid couldn't fail.

There was only one little problem. All his equipment was on his uniform belt, which, of course, he wasn't wearing while he was undercover. He couldn't get started, he couldn't even dust that rather obvious knife for fingerprints...

"Damn!" he growled to himself.

"What?" Dariya questioned, suddenly nervous. If there was a problem with this much evidence that was all so obvious, then there wasn't much chance of finding anything better. Were their hopes lost already?

"I need some stuff, but I left it at the hotel..." he admitted.

"Then go back and get it, quickly!" she urged.

"But then we'll have to find another opportunity to get back down here. How likely are we do get another chance?" Antonin asked uncertainly.

Dariya considered this, then shook her head, "We won't, not today. He'll be down here as soon as he gets up. We'll have to get the stuff today and come back tomorrow."

Antonin looked at the pile of disturbing 'evidence'. Then thought of Sunnikov's words and his own suspicions. No, if they had this huge case and it had taken them this long to get anywhere, then the Volkovs must have a pretty useful dirty cop somewhere in Yaroslavl. Meaning he didn't know how long it would be until they were tipped off that the investigation was happening again.

"We might not have time to wait until tomorrow!" he groaned.

Dariya bit her lip and tried to think, "Okay... So, what do you need?"

"I need fingerprint powder, a camera, my police notebook and... Screw it, just those essentials, that'll do if we don't have time," Antonin decided.

"Right, so if we can't risk leaving and having to wait until tomorrow, you stay here and I'll go." Dariya told him.

Antonin looked sceptical, "And if someone finds me?"

"They won't. I'll lock the door and take the key with me," she assured him.

So... You'll lock me in the creepy basement full of rotting corpses and go and take my stuff? Antonin thought. Great plan.

But it wasn't as though he had a better one. Besides, if he couldn't trust her, who could he trust?

"Alright then. Here..." he dug a slip of paper out of his pocket with his hotel room's address on it, "It should all be there. Just tell them you're visiting me and get in and out as fast as you can. The stuff should be with my uniform, so check the closet." he instructed her.

Dariya tucked the piece of paper into her pocket hastily, "Got it!" she nodded, "Wish me luck,"

"Good luck!" he replied sincerely.

She nodded and slipped away through the basement, disappearing up the stairs.

Antonin edged away from the bodies, found a workbench that was empty and sat down to wait, hoping Dariya could move with speed and get the tools to finish this grim job. It was turning out to be a lot less of an adventure and more of a nightmare.

Footsteps faded away above him and were replaced with the sound of the door slamming shut, then the click of it locking behind Dariya. Now all he could do was wait. And hope to God that there wasn't a spare key anywhere in this awful place so that he would at least know that the unlocking of the door meant she had made it back.

But until the door unlocked again, he would just have to sit and wonder if he had done the right thing by letting her shut him in here and leave.

THE 'MOVING IN' MISSION

Dariya shut the door behind her, turned the key in the lock, then slipped into her pocket carefully and checked her watch. Damn, she really didn't have much time. Her knowledge of her father's routine indicated that he would already be up. He'd go and have breakfast, and then... Then he would notice that something was wrong.

She was relying on his arrogance to do the rest. He would, she hoped, assume that no one could have possibly infiltrated his precious workshop without his knowledge and that the issue was, therefore, a stuck lock. Which gave her and Antonin however long it took him to fix the lock. She knew he wouldn't do that himself. He'd get Valeria, her expert lockpicker sister, to do it for him. And at this time in the morning, Valeria would be otherwise engaged in her usual round of fighting with Vladlena.

Both girls insisted this was only for practice, but really, they were at each other's throats every day. Normally, Dariya despaired of the fact that none of her family members appeared to make any effort to get along, but today it served her purpose.

Because she calculated, it would take her father another five minutes to finish his breakfast, five to notice the lock and alert Valeria, and at least thirty for Valeria to stop fighting. Then properly about fifteen for her to get it open.

Which gave her and Antonin fifty-five minutes in total. Given that he had to document everything, that wasn't much time. But it was the best chance they were likely to get, so she just had to be fast and hope her calculations were correct.

She hadn't gone into all this detail when revealing her plan to Antonin. He was clearly already worried about their tense situation. She didn't want to cause him to panic. Granted, right now that left *her* doing all the panicking, as she tried to speed-walk along the corridor, wanting to get on with her mission, without running and drawing attention.

It shouldn't be too hard to get through the house without anyone becoming suspicious. She wasn't likely to encounter anyone until she got back to the living room, and if they started asking questions, she would just tell them she was helping Antonin move in, as she had promised to, then go about her business as quickly as she could.

She nodded to herself as she reaffirmed this plan in her head, trying to use it to calm herself down. I'm okay, I've got a plan...

The door ahead of her opened suddenly and Vladimir stepped out of the living room and walked towards her.

The panic was back instantly. She had never felt so trapped by the sight of her own father before, but now she felt as though guilt was written all over her and there was no way to get away. And, at the back of her panicking mind, the still-thinking part of her brain realised that his sudden arrival meant her calculations were wrong and they had a lot less time than she had first thought.

That only made the panic worse. She stared at her approaching father with silent horror, which she hoped wasn't as obvious as it felt right now.

"Morning, Dariya, Dear," her father beamed at her, apparently oblivious to her terror. "What are you doing out here at breakfast time?"

The question seemed innocent and his smile was still bright, but his eyes were suddenly hard and suspicious. Was she not supposed to be here? She glanced around out of the corners of her eyes, trying not to be too obvious as she searched desperately for an excuse.

The rows of doors around them stared back at her impassively.

One door, identical to all the others yet known to her, threw up an excuse, and she blurted it out hastily, "Just... Just showing Antonin where the bathroom is!" It was a poor excuse, but it was the only one she had.

Vladimir raised an eyebrow, "Wouldn't the one upstairs be more convenient?" he questioned. His voice was calm and cool. He wasn't accusing her of anything. But the doubt was there, underpinning all of his questions.

She hated it. It made her feel as though he knew something. "...It was occupied!" she answered him hastily again, before moving on, "Anyway, I better go and get started on the moving!"

Again, there was a slightly surprised look from her father, "You're not waiting for him?"

"He asked me to get started without him. I know where he was staying and where all his stuff is, so I will handle it," she answered.

"I see," Vladimir nodded and walked on, passing her by calmly.

Inwardly, Dariya breathed a sigh of relief. There, no more questions. She had finally satisfied him enough for this interrogation to end.

She began to walk away from him, heading out.

He stopped and spoke up behind her, "In that case, I'll come along and help you," he told her in a friendly tone.

She froze, thankful that he couldn't see her face right now because this time she knew she couldn't hide her horror.

It wasn't an offer, in spite of his light tone. He was monitoring her now, and she would have to be quick to slip anything past him.

As his footsteps started to come towards her again, she forced her face out of its frozen rictus and into a smile, "Good idea, thank you!" she trilled as innocently as possible, while behind her smile, her mind raced for a way to accomplish her task without him noticing.

"No problem," he answered sweetly, catching up to her and walking along with her.

The father-daughter duo walked along in relative silence to the hotel. Dariya wandered along awkwardly, hoping Vladimir didn't start asking her more questions, but he was mercifully quiet.

It didn't take them long to reach the place, make their excuses at the desk and hurry up to Antonin's room before any further questions were asked.

"Right," Vladimir began as they stepped into the room, "Where do we start?"

Dariya crossed to the wardrobe, "Clothes should be the easiest thing to move, right? Let's get them out of the way and come back for anything bigger or more awkward," she suggested, needing to locate Antonin's uniform as he had instructed her.

And, she realised suddenly as Vladimir nodded and moved to help her, she had to find it before her father did. He had some strong opinions about the police. Namely that they should all be killed. He had gone into quite graphic detail on that subject many, many times.

Glancing down, she saw an empty travel bag at the bottom of the wardrobe and grabbed it, ready to shove anything incriminating - In her father's warped opinion, anyway - out of sight. Now she just had to find it...

A flash of light glinting off something gold caught her eye and she lunged forward, catching hold of the source and checking to confirm her suspicions. Yes, the light had been shining off his police badge.

She glanced at her father. He was lingering by the door, waiting to see if she needed help. Thank God he hadn't charged in to 'help' regardless. She thrust the uniform into the bag and piled other clothes on top hastily until she couldn't cram anymore in.

"Alright, first load done!" she told him cheerfully, "Do you want to run back home with this lot while I stay here and get more ready?" she suggested, hoping that would allow her to hide anything else that was 'suspicious' before he was back.

But Vladimir seemed to have something on his mind. He was staring at the floor as though he was transfixed. "Hm... No, I think it'll be better if you go back, Sweetheart. I can handle things here."

Dariya knew there was no point in arguing with him. Even if the argument was over something seemingly trivial like this, it never ended well. He insisted on things going his way, all the time.

She just had to hope that Antonin had been right, and all of his police stuff was with his uniform, safely stashed in the bag.

At least she had time to get these to him, so he could get to work while Vladimir was out of the picture.

She gave her father a quick nod and hurried out before he could say anything else and ruin her plans all over again. He seemed to have a knack for completely screwing all her plans up. It was as though he knew what she was thinking, though she hoped he didn't, otherwise her days were numbered.

Pushing that rather grim thought away, she scurried back to the house and ran to her room. Inside, she threw down the bag and delved into it. Tugging the uniform from the bottom, she fiddled with all the compartments on his belt and his pockets, checking all the equipment he had asked for was there.

When she realised it was, she sighed in relief. Somehow, she had managed it even with her father breathing down her neck. Now she just had to get the stuff to Antonin. She grabbed another, smaller bag, this time from her own wardrobe, thrust it in, and headed downstairs.

Unlocking the door, she hurried down, hoping Antonin was alright. Her plan must have been hard on him, leaving him shut in that horrible place, but it had been the only way she could think of keeping one of them able to access the evidence and getting the things they needed.

As she reached the bottom of the stairs, she heard him sigh in relief.

"You're back, great!" he smiled, thankful to see her and know the plan had worked.

"Here's your uniform," Dariya pulled it out and thrust it at him. "Everything's here. Now I better go again..." she added, thinking of her father rummaging through Antonin's belongings.

"Thanks!" he beamed gratefully, knowing how much he needed the tools that she had smuggled to him, "But why do you have to go back?" he frowned. She had said everything was there, after all.

Dariya sighed, "Papa asked what I was doing. I said I was helping you move. He insisted on helping, so I guess we're putting all your stuff in my room for now..."

Antonin shrugged, "Okay, I guess, if it keeps him from getting suspicious."

"I hope it will," Dariya nodded, "Good luck with your work," she called to him as she began to depart again.

He smiled, waving to her as she left before he turned to the evidence and got started.

Dariya arrived back at the hotel a little too late, otherwise, she might have found her father's behaviour odd, and become more alert.

Vladimir crossed the room to the wardrobe, stooped and picked something shiny off the floor. He glowered at it as he turned it over in his hands, then pocketed it. Then he turned away from the wardrobe and began to look through the drawers instead.

It was only when he heard Dariya's hand on the door handle that he slammed the drawer he was looking through shut and hurried back to the wardrobe, continuing where she had left off.

So, she didn't see anything and entered a perfectly normal scene. So, there was never any warning.

THE ATTACK

Vladimir and Dariya continued to work in silence. Dariya didn't speak for nervousness. Her mind was currently full of worries about Antonin. She could only hope that he was able to get his work done with speed, but without drawing any attention from her siblings.

And then she was worried about what might happen afterwards. It would be a bittersweet victory. Her father would be taken from her and would no doubt be full of anger, swearing vengeance. He may even try to mobilise the rest of the family to enact that vengeance. But at least her own fate would finally be in her own hands. She could choose to travel and go where they couldn't hurt her.

Perhaps she would follow Antonin. They had only known each other for such a short time, but he had shown her more love and support than anyone else, and so she was growing very close to him, thinking of him almost as a brother of sorts. After all, he had taught her that one could choose who was 'family', and she needed a better family than her own.

Vladimir's silence was different. He was distracted, deep in thought. There was something horribly wrong... He had worked so hard to build this city into something great that would serve his every need. And now, at the heart of it, there was a festering infection.

He had been... Working on getting rid of the city's rather persistent police department for a little while, but he had decided to take his time, while they could still serve a purpose. After all, *some* of them could be persuaded to be useful.

This was different. An outsider had barged in on his territory and threatened to take all his hard work away.

Of course, he had known for a long time of the Chief's plan to get other people involved. At the time, this had not worried him. He'd thought he would easily identify the person as soon as they set foot in Yaroslavl. They would never survive. *That,* of course, was the point. Someone whom he could easily identify and take down would no doubt throw a spanner in the operation against him. The death of a police officer, made to look like an accident, would confuse the authorities and mean more paperwork for them to go through. Meanwhile, he'd be left alone.

It had very nearly worked. On the way into the hotel, he noticed the white spatter on the back of a car parked outside and nodded to himself. It had added up neatly with the tip-off he had received from his 'friend' in the police department.

But his spy was clearly a coward. Too weighed down with doing things quietly and subtly, never actually getting their own hands dirty... They could have easily just given him Antonin's identity. Instead, they had played games with him, marking a car, sneaking around, trying to draw the process out so they could demand more money from him.

That was hardly the point though. He could deal with them later. Antonin was his most pressing concern. The man had crept into his operation, hidden the signs away and, most disgustingly of all, seduced his poor, innocent daughter.

He ground his teeth in frustration as he glanced over at Dariya. Yes, that was it. His child had been treasured, carefully raised... She would never betray him; despite the stupid rumours he had heard. Instead, she had *been* betrayed.

That only added to Antonin's list of crimes. The first was being an outsider, a Muscovite in *his* city, the second was being a *police officer.* He felt the badge he had discovered earlier, still sitting in his pocket and wished that metal could tear, for he longed to destroy it. Police officers were always the enemy, for they would never understand why he was special, above their petty laws.

But the third crime was most serious. Antonin was interfering with his family, the one thing that he needed most to achieve his goal, the warriors that would one day be the jewel in his crowd... That was tainting something sacred to him. It was unforgivable.

He was pleased that he had, at last, caught the intruder, and that he had been the one to discover the badge. Dariya wouldn't have to face Antonin's betrayal just yet, and when the time came, he would be there to reassure her. He could reiterate his lessons about not trusting outsiders...

But for now, he had to take the horrible little man down. He let his fury take over and stormed out of the hotel room, determined to find Antonin and put an end to his treachery before it harmed the family.

Mystified and alarmed by her father's sudden anger, Dariya abandoned her task too and hurried after him.

Antonin was hurrying too, moving quickly as he took fingerprints from the weapons he found with the corpses. The knife wasn't the only one, after all. One body had a syringe shoved into the throat; another still had an axe embedded in the back... He took prints for them all, vaguely wondering how many weapons these people had and why they had been so dumb to leave them with the bodies. Unless this was some kind of weird shrine to their murderous nature... But that puzzle wasn't why he was here.

With the fingerprints recorded, he took his camera out and snapped some pictures to show what he had found. He made sure to take some notes in his book as well, loathed as he was to record all the gory details, it was sadly necessary.

He double-checked the records, then stepped away from the bodies. Shutting the door behind him, he decided to leave things as he had found them, just in case someone came looking before he could get the records to the police station and start further action.

That meant he had to leave nothing out of place... He was hesitant to approach the machine Dariya had revealed earlier - Something about Vladimir's 'inventions' chilled him, even though they weren't against the law, and so technically weren't his business - But he had to. He pulled the sheet over it hastily and walked away, watching the thing warily in case it did something.

When nothing terrible happened, he gave a small sigh of relief. It was over, his dealings in this creepy old basement with these frankly disturbed people were finally over. He could walk away, leaving the local police to arrest Vladimir.

And he would have made good his promise to Dariya, restoring her freedom.

So, he could go home and make good his promise to Nikolina as well. He was really missing her.

But the thought that all this was soon to be over lifted his spirits as he headed up the stairs. He hadn't heard Dariya lock the door upon her second exit since her father - The only person likely to go down to the basement - Was out of the way.

He was glad she had thought of that. He didn't want to delay making his report any longer. He slipped out and hurried through the house, hoping to avoid a collision with any of the Volkovs.

He was in luck; the corridor ahead was empty. He hurried through it and into the living room, which was also deserted. Not much further now, he assured himself as he grabbed the handle of the hall door, pushing it open.

At the same time, Vladimir shoved the front door open and ran down the narrow entrance hall, rushing directly at him.

Bewildered and alarmed, he tried to move to the side, but the older man tackled him, pushing him to the ground with a thump.

He groaned, shutting his eyes briefly on the impact. When he opened them again, he glanced past Vladimir's eyes, which hovered before his, burning with a white-hot rage, and saw a stunned Dariya standing in the doorway, staring at them.

His view of her began to blur, and it was only then that he realised Vladimir's hand was tightening around his throat.

RESCUE?

Struggling to claw Vladimir's fingers away from his skin, Antonin could hear the other man laughing.

"You really thought you could stop me? You're going to die, and your pathetic police friends won't find your body. They never found the others!" he mocked.

Even though he was gasping for breath, Antonin kept face by cursing at the other man. Inside though, he was shaken-up and scared. How had Vladimir found out about his job? Did whatever corrupt police officer that was helping him work that fast, or had Dariya betrayed him?

He didn't like either idea one little bit, but right now, his main priority was living long enough to find the truth, and that was becoming a challenge in itself. He was feeling very light-headed now, and breathing was a struggle.

He tried to focus, his eyes still blurred and his hearing seeming distant...

He could hear the faint sound of running footsteps. Air rushed past him. Air. That would be great right now. He tugged at the hand around his throat weakly and tried to breathe, gasping loudly.

He could hear Vladimir's mocking tone of voice, but he could no longer focus on the words. Somewhere, a long way off, a series of clatters rang out. The part of his mind that was still able to think through the dizziness and pain wondered what was happening.

The hand around his throat briefly relaxed, indicating confusion from his opponent too. But it wasn't enough for him to free himself. Vladimir wouldn't allow himself to be distracted for long. Antonin swore internally. He had had one tiny chance, and he had missed it. Now the man's grip seemed tighter than ever, and he couldn't hold out any longer. The light was starting to fade, his blurry vision leaving him altogether now.

The last thing he remembered was another sound, distant in his ringing ears...

BANG!

Dariya waited a few minutes and then nervously pushed the door open a crack, peeking through.

The fog had cleared now, and she could see them. Both men were slumped on the floor, showing no apparent signs of life.

Just as she had planned.

She finally walked out into the room and approached them. Vladimir had collapsed on top of Antonin, and she stooped over them, taking her father by his arms and, with considerable effort, heaving him off the other man.

His lack of complaints, as well as the lack of comment from Antonin, confirmed her hopes. She had rendered them both unconscious. She could feel her father's pulse under her fingers, and Antonin's chest was rising and falling gently, so she was reassured that they had at least survive the process.

Now she just had to decide what to do with them, and quickly, before any of her siblings responded to the explosion sound.

It had unfortunately been necessary. She had been at a loss to help Antonin without attracting her father's attention... Then she had remembered one of his 'experiments' that he had boasted about a while ago.

He had created a grenade that would render anyone nearby unconscious.

As soon as she had remembered that, she had fled to his workshop, hearing his smug words about his daughter being 'safe now' ringing out behind her as he continued to battle with Antonin.

It hadn't taken her long to find the grenades, but she had been nervous to use them. Her father vastly over-estimated his own intelligence, when in actual fact his 'inventions' often went wrong.

But it wasn't like she had a choice. She had to act now or lose her only hope at freedom and her first real friend at once. So, she had secreted herself in the next room and thrown the grenade. Hiding behind the door so that it wouldn't affect her too, she'd hoped for the best. To her surprise, it had worked.

For the next part of her plan, she eventually decided on dragging her father to his own precious basement and leaving him. It was easier said than done. He was heavier than he looked. In the end, she hauled him as far as the door, shoved him through and locked it.

No doubt when he woke up, he'd find a spare key, let himself out and then rampage around looking for whoever was to blame, but she hoped he wouldn't realise what had actually happened.

So, she left him there and returned to Antonin. When she got there, one of her brothers was standing over him with a bemused look.

"What happened to him? There was a bang..." he said.

Dariya smiled to herself. They had heard, but thankfully, they had sent Dmitri to investigate. Dmitri was her favourite brother, a kind soul. But he wasn't the brightest spark, leaving him vulnerable to the others bossing him around.

She had always wanted to teach him to stand up to them but had been too nervous herself. But for once, she was grateful for his willingness to believe what he was told.

"He fainted. The bang was him falling," she lied.

"Oh... I hope he's okay," Dmitri replied.

"He will be, Dima," she assured him.

Accepting this with a nod, her brother trotted off dutifully, probably back to whoever had sent him. She looked down at Antonin. It was probably not a good idea for him to be here when her father woke up. But how where they going to get anywhere else in time?

She couldn't exactly move very quickly if she had to drag him with her... Her only chance was the car. Fortunately, her father kept the car keys on the living room table and let them all use it for whatever tasks he had given them.

*Un*fortunately, she couldn't legally drive. She hated to break the law, feeling it made her no better than her father.

But right now, her friend's life was in danger. And it wasn't as though she was going far.

Reluctantly, she grabbed the car keys from the table and pocketed them, before dragging Antonin to the hallway. She paused to gather her strength and pulled him to the front door.

Opening it cautiously, she looked around for anyone who might see.

Two of her father's hired guards watched the front of the house with an air of boredom. They were simply a showing off tactic, paid to boost the old man's ego even further. They never did any real work. No one around here would ever dare attack the house.

Fortunately, they were the only people around. She supposed she should have anticipated that. The locals tended to avoid this area if they could, just in case. And the guards were either paid well enough or disinterested enough to turn a blind eye to just about *anything.*

She finally could finally stop worrying about how suspicious she undoubtedly looked as she dragged Antonin's slumbering body out of the house and to the car. She opened the back door, lifted his feet onto the seats and shoved him inside. It wasn't the careful and dignified way she would like her friend to be handled, but she didn't have much choice. She couldn't lift his entire body at once.

It wasn't as secure as she would have liked either, but she didn't have time to worry about that. She slammed the door, jumped into the driver's seat and took off, driving as fast as she dared, which was about thirty miles per hour.

It was fortunate that the local police station wasn't far away.

AFTERMATH

Waking up shirtless in the back of a strange car gave Antonin quite a jolt. The last thing he could remember was fighting with Vladimir... He rubbed his throat tentatively. It still hurt.

He must have passed out as the other man choked him, but what had happened since then? Someone appeared to have taken off the baggy hooded jacket he had been wearing as a shirt, which was bad news because he had, in order to get the evidence past the Volkovs, resorted to bundling his uniform up underneath it. For once, he had been grateful for the fact that his mother's 'care packages' always consisted of ill-fitting clothes and his own lack of care when dressing.

But his plan had failed, and his missing uniform still carried all of his important equipment, and so wherever it was - Presumably with his stolen shirt - The evidence was there too.

The obvious answer was Vladimir. He must have stolen it

while he was unconscious! That thought shook him to his core, though, because it meant Dariya had definitely betrayed him. Vladimir could have uncovered his secret by complete accident, but he wouldn't know about the evidence without her input...

He'd thought he could trust her after all they had done together, but now he wished he had never believed that. Though... If she had betrayed him, her plan seemed like a strange one. Why reveal all her secrets first?

She could have lied to him, he supposed. She admitted to being a practised liar... But the inner workings of Dariya's mind were a puzzle he would have to figure out later. Right now, he faced a much more important problem - Where the hell was, he and how was he going to get out of here?

Clearly, he was in the back of someone's car... They were probably taking him somewhere where he wouldn't be found. Though it could be useful to know where they took their victims, he didn't fancy hanging around to find out.

Especially since there were two options: Either he was assumed to be dead after Vladimir attacked him, and they had searched him for anything important, then intended to dispose of his 'body' with a little more ceremony than they had the others, or they knew he was alive and were keeping him for some other, doubtlessly sinister reason.

Neither being disposed of nor being their prisoner appealed to him. So, he sat up and tried the obvious route out first, fiddling with the door. It was locked, but fortunately, unlocked from the inside with the push of a button. Well, if he was being kidnapped, that was a rather stupid oversight, he thought to himself, still smug about his escape.

He opened the door and climbed out of the car, only to see someone bearing down on him from across the car park. His attacker was apparently wearing his own hoodie.

Whoever this person was, they must be responsible for his current situation. It was probably one of the Volkovs.

That thought made him freeze up for a moment, but he jolted himself out of it hastily. There was no time to panic, he just had to run before they could reach him. There was no time. Upon seeing him, they had begun to run towards him and were now nearly on top of him.

"What are you doing, idiot?! Get back in the damn car!" Dariya's familiar voice was amplified now as she screamed at him, trying to grab him.

He pulled away from her, "What the hell?! Why would I listen to *you?!" he* flung his words back at her accusingly, still stung by her betrayal.

He heard her gasp of shock before she managed to stifle it. She seemed genuinely surprised. Perhaps she hadn't expected him to figure it out so quickly. Then she pulled herself together, responding in anger rather than letting him see her shock and hurt.

"Why listen to me? Maybe because I'm the only one in this whole city who bothered to try and save your sorry ass!"

He snorted derisively. Oh, she was convincing, but hadn't she convinced him once before? Not this time.

"Save me? How is letting your psycho father choke me half to death, then stealing half my stuff and locking me in your car 'saving' me?!"

Her response to that was quick and decisive. She slapped him, *hard.* He'd never expected a small young woman to hit so hard, but there was a lot of emotion behind the blow, and it rocked him, stunning him into silence, despite his own anger. It seemed to stun her, too. For a moment, she stood staring at the red mark she had left on his cheek. Then she turned away, blushing at the awkwardness of the situation, but still seething too.

"Just... Just get in the car and we can talk about this privately..." she muttered.

Antonin looked at her in disbelief. Like he was going to just get back into her car!

Then he looked around and it began to dawn on him where they were. They had been yelling at one another, about extremely private issues, in the middle of a public car park. Which, he noted, seeing the building in the background for the first time, appeared to be the car park to Yaroslavl's Police Station.

Why would Dariya have brought him here if she had been kidnapping him on her father's behalf? The voice of doubt slipped into his mind. Maybe she was worth listening to after all.

Silent and red with embarrassment that he had only just thought of this, he slipped back into the car through the still-open back door and sat down quietly.

Dariya took a breath, composing herself again, then opened the front door and sat in the driver's seat. Once both the doors were shut and they had both taken a few minutes, she finally spoke.

"I'm sorry I hit you. But you hurt me, not believing me. I really was trying to help..." She tried to explain.

Antonin nodded mournfully. She seemed as though she was on the verge of tears, and he regretted not stopping to listen to her sooner. But in the heat of the moment, he had let his thoughts guide him.

Often, that worked. His quick-thinking and ability to jump to conclusions based on evidence made him a good policeman, but every once in a while, it went wrong.

He had jumped to the *wrong* conclusion, and let his emotions take over from there.

"I'm sorry too. I should have listened. I just couldn't understand what had happened to get me from fighting your father at your house, to being locked in the back of a car..." he admitted.

It was Dariya's turn to nod her understanding and realise she hadn't considered the other side either. "I guess that would seem suspicious. But I promise I didn't mean you any harm!" she clarified.

"I see that now," Antonin agreed, feeling ready to trust her again now that he had calmed down and heard her out, "But at the time... I was hurt at the idea that you *might* do that. I felt we were friends."

Dariya turned in her seat and smiled at him. He was taken aback to see tears shining in her eyes. The whole ordeal had clearly upset her, "We *are* friends!" she insisted passionately.

"And so, you helped me somehow?" he asked, touched that she would do that, but still confused as to exactly what had happened.

She wiped her eyes, "Sorry, this has just been... A lot to deal with," she commented, before trying again, "Anyway, yeah, I helped you. I had to. Papa was going to kill you! Fortunately, I used one of his inventions against him. Knock-out grenades. Put you both to sleep and shut him out of the way, then brought you here," she revealed.

She paused, then looked down and realised she was still wearing his hoodie, "Oh! Yeah, I also handed your evidence in. I had to.

Now that Papa's onto you, we don't have much time. It took me a while to find it, and I also needed a disguise," she gestured to the hoodie, the hood of which practically covered her face, "My father probably has some low-level officers snooping around for him. I can't be seen around her. Besides, thanks to him, I'm a 'suspicious person' to most police officers. Thankfully, once I got in and got to see her, the Chief was very understanding. I explained everything."

"Wow..." Antonin murmured. He hadn't expected her to go up against her own father, even indirectly, to save his life, let alone take the huge risk of continuing his job while he was decommissioned. "Thank you! I mean it, thanks to you, we might still be able to pull this off!"

Dariya's eyes shone with joy this time, "I know right! And I saved your ass on top of that!"

Just as they started to laugh, she remembered something and instantly sobered up, "...Seriously though, I wasn't being weird when I told you to get in the car. You're gonna want to keep a low profile and hope this case is finished soon. Pretty sure my father's not going to give up after one attempt on your life."

Antonin sighed. "I guess every silver lining comes with a cloud. We'll just have to hope Chief Sunnikov can handle it. I'll find somewhere to lay low, in case I'm needed again. I'm only going back to Moscow when Vladimir's safely in prison," he added determinedly.

"You might be here a while then. I'll find somewhere for you to stay," Dariya told him.

He nodded thoughtfully. He'd need somewhere to hide if Vladimir was looking for him, but he couldn't abandon the case altogether, not now he had been through so much and come so close.

HIDING OUT

Antonin spent most of the rest of that day sitting in the car while Dariya took over. She drove to the hotel and checked him out, then took him somewhere else. He wasn't entirely sure where it was, she just drove down some side roads. Endless twists and turns eventually led them to a large grey building. It looked a lot like an abandoned warehouse.

Dariya stopped the car. "Wait here, I have to check something," she told him, before getting out.

Time seemed to pass very slowly, and he began to wonder what she was doing. Why would she have to check something? If it wasn't safe already, then why had she brought him here?

He had expected 'somewhere to lay low' to be another hotel or something, but the more he thought about it, the less sense it made. The local hotels would be the first places Vladimir would look for him. No one was likely to look for him here. Even he didn't really know where 'here' was, after all. So, it was the perfect hiding spot.

But he still hated it. He hated hiding, acting like a fugitive when he was the one in the right. And he was still confused by the nature of this place and what Dariya was preparing.He had to accept it though, he had to sit tight and wait for her because the Volkovs really did run this city. They would hunt him down.

The only other place to go was home. But this wasn't over. It wouldn't be over until arrests were made and the case had been through court. He couldn't abandon it now, even if he *was* in danger. So, he had to go along with whatever Dariya's plan was and hope it worked out for the best.

She soon re-emerged and nodded to him. "It's alright, I just wanted to make sure the power still works. It's been abandoned for a while and I didn't want to leave you without power at all," she explained.

He could understand that. If he was going to have to be here for a while, he didn't want to be stuck in the dark all the time, "And it's connected?" he checked.

"Yeah," she nodded again, "All connected. Lights still work. I checked the water in the toilet too, so you have that. I'll bring some food and bedding over when I get a chance."

Well, it looked like he was going to be living with just the essentials for a while... He tried not to mind too much. In his current position, it was good of her to find him somewhere to live and provide for him at all. Especially after their recent argument.

"Thanks," he smiled as graciously as he could, finally getting out of the car. "I guess I'll go in and get settled. I'll see you... Whenever you can come," he added, feeling a little sad to be saying goodbye to her.

It would probably be the longest that he had been separated from her for the mission, and he had grown quite close to her by now. Certainly, she seemed to be his only friend around here. But of course, she couldn't stay. Her family would ask awkward questions...

She appeared to understand, giving him a sad smile, "I'll try not to be too long. Stay safe!"

He watched her get back into the car and drive away before he went inside. His new safehouse was indeed an abandoned warehouse and so was pretty bare. But at least he knew he was safe here. He also had the luxury of space. He could easily walk around inside, which was better than he had expected. In a hotel, he would have probably been holed up in a single room for however long. True, a room would have provided more comfort than this huge expanse of empty space.

There really was nothing in here besides the damp on the walls, the tiny side room where there were a toilet and a tiny sink that was inhabited by a whole civilisation of spiders. He turned on the strip lights. They were glaring, but he had had quite enough of being shut up in the dark after investigating Vladimir's dingy basement.

After that, he had exhausted the things that he could do, so he sat on the cold, hard ground and waited for Dariya's return.

While he waited, he reflected on his recent experiences.

The week had started so well, with his first-ever solo assignment and his proposal to Nikolina. It had been so full of potential and hope for the future. He had seen himself and Lina doing well in their jobs, getting promotions, settling down together and having kids.

Perhaps that was boring and predictable, but he was beginning to see that the adventurous life wasn't as much fun as it seemed in films. It was certainly a lot more stressful and a lot more painful. He had been expecting blazing guns and wild car chases, out of which he would emerge - A fearless hero - unscathed. He hadn't expected to be afraid for his life, hiding away like this, with bruises around his throat and dangerous people on his trail.

He wished he could go back home and immerse him in 'boring' paperwork with Ilya. Or listen to Ekaterina and Sasha squabble while he tried to eat his breakfast. But most of all, he wished he could be with Nikolina. He wanted to find out how her case went, what she was up to, what plans she had for their wedding.

But he still felt he had to be conscientious and finish the case he had started. Besides, Dariya had helped him out so much and was banking on him to help her out too. He owed it to her to stay until she was free from her father's grasp, then... Well, then she could make her own life for herself and he would just stay in touch, like a good friend.

When it came down to it, he realised, people didn't do dangerous jobs to be movie-style superheroes. He wasn't a superhero, nor were any of the other cops he knew. Ilya did this kind of thing to take care of his kids, he was out here doing it to help Dariya and so that he could go back and start his own family.

Ordinary people like him and Ilya did dangerous jobs because they wanted to look out for their friends and families. He smiled to himself, cheering up a little. Perhaps that was a better motivation, after all. Don't try to save the world, just focus on the bits of it that are worth saving.

These thoughts kept him in good spirits, even though he was in a pretty bleak situation at the moment.

And Dariya helped, for she was good to her word and returned the next day with a small portable stove, some provisions that he could prepare on it and some bedding.

She also brought news, "Things aren't going too badly at the moment. I've managed to convince my father that he passed out during the fight and I moved him so you couldn't attack him again. He doesn't suspect me. I also told him I didn't know what happened to you... I thought about saying you died, but then he'd want to see your body," she explained.

"Well, at least he doesn't hate you now as well. Though I take it he's still looking for me?" he responded, taking the news as a mixed blessing, Dariya wasn't in danger, but he wasn't off the hook yet.

"Oh, yeah. He's practically obsessed with it. He's got loads of people out hunting you down. But you'll be safe here," she tried to reassure him after breaking that bit of bad news.

"And it shouldn't be too long until he gets arrested..." Antonin cheered himself up with that thought.

Dariya looked a little sceptical. "I don't know, we haven't seen any signs of activity yet..."

"It won't be instant or obvious," Antonin told her, "But don't worry. It's bound to happen now. It's been coming for a while, all they needed was evidence. There's no way he'll get away this time."

THE TRAITOR

Antonin's days ticked by in relative peace, if not boredom. Nothing seemed to be happening, which became very frustrating. He had been through a lot to get to the point where the police could take Vladimir Volkov down and now, they were wasting time.

Frustration gave way to suspicion as time passed. He was beginning to think that either something had gone wrong when he had recorded the evidence and Dariya had turned in it, or Yaroslavl's corruption problem went a lot further than he had realised.

He couldn't really do anything right now though. He was effectively a wanted man. Dariya had warned him that going outside was bound to get him killed. So, he was stuck with nothing to do but wait, his frustration and suspicion growing by the day.

Dariya wasn't finding things any easier. She might not be stuck in an abandoned warehouse, fearing for her life, but she was stuck at home, listening to her father rant.

Vladimir had deployed most of his children to hunt for Antonin across the city, but Dariya was kept at home to 'help' him with plans that he had. So far, she hadn't discovered the nature of his plans because he had spent the time ranting and raving. She just tuned most of it out, but it didn't stop him.

Currently, she was sitting at the dining table, eating lunch, while her father paced up and down the room, spitting fire.

"How dare that slimy little maggot come here and interfere with our business?! He lied to you just to spy on us!" he growled.

"I know..." Dariya sighed. Her sigh was mostly one of boredom. She had heard this far too many times.

Vladimir, in his emotional state, mistook it for sadness and shook his head, "I am so sorry, my dear, how were you supposed to know? To think, he could have destroyed all of us, if I hadn't accompanied you and saved you!"

She rolled her eyes while he wasn't looking. He was just using this as extra fuel for his stories about how brilliant he was and how she should just stay around him, where she would be safe, forever. It would just be another excuse for him to control her life. She could already hear him starting up again, his rants a familiar backtrack for her thoughts.

Eventually, she couldn't tune him out anymore and decided it was time to interject. That could be a risky business, knowing his temper, but at this point, all she wanted was to shut him up.

"Papa, really, it's not as though any harm's been done. I expect all he did was run away. He's probably long gone by now," she tried to pacify him.

It was too much to hope that he would buy it and leave Antonin in peace, but if she was calm and tried to be the voice of reason, she might get beyond the ranting and find out how much he knew.

She had already uncovered how he had found out about Antonin's job, but she wanted to know all the details, just in case there was anything that could help her friend, or at least keep him out of danger.

"No harm? My dear, naïve little Dariya," she gritted her teeth at her father's dramatic, patronising tone, "That man could have toppled my whole brilliant organisation and ruined everything! And I know he's still in town... I *will* find him."

With every word, he made her hate him more. But already, she was learning new information. He knew Antonin was still in town. How?

The best way to uncover more seemed to be to make him think he had to explain the twisted-up workings of his mind to her. When he had thought she 'didn't understand', he had inadvertently let something useful slip.

So, she wrinkled her brow at him, feigning confusion. "How would he have done that? Anyway, there's no way to be sure that he's still around... Surely he'd go back to Moscow?"

Vladimir seemed angry at the reminder of how his whole precious operation could have been destroyed. "He broke into my workshop! He could have done so much damage!" he cried out in fury. "And of course, he's still creeping around here! His car's still at the hotel!"

Dariya stopped. She didn't want to make her father any crosser and risk endangering herself. If he suspected her, he'd surely kill her.

Besides, she had learnt a disturbing amount. Vladimir definitely had someone more powerful than she had suspected working for him.

She hadn't even known Antonin *had* a car here, but Vladimir had it under observation. And how could he know about Antonin accessing the workshop? They hadn't broken in; it had all been done very neatly. He couldn't possibly know.

Unless...

Her heart skipped a beat as the thought crept into her brain. There *was* a way for him to know. If he had seen the evidence. She could only think of two possible chances for him to have seen it. He could have looked while he had been fighting Antonin, but he had been focused on killing the other man and hadn't stopped to think or to search him.

The only other way for him to know would be if one of his spies was the person who she had entrusted their vital evidence to. The one person Antonin had had any dealings with in Yaroslavl, other than herself. The one person who would know all the details of this entire case.

The Chief of Police.

It was a horrible thought, but it made too much sense. If the Chief of Police was being paid by her father, it would explain why no local case against any member of her family had ever stuck. They were always dropped or overturned.

But its current implications were much, much more serious. Her heart had leapt into her mouth. She had to go to Antonin and tell him about her suspicion right now. If she was working for

Vladimir, then he was in more danger than they had realised. Her father had access to much more information than they realised. And he had someone in his organisation who could easily dispose of their precious evidence, waste all their hard work and destroy Antonin's case.

Without a case to help him get rid of Vladimir, Antonin had nothing to potentially protect him from the wrath of the Volkov family.

More and more dark thoughts swirled in Dariya's stricken mind and she knew she had to act now if she wanted to help her only friend survive.

"I see," she nodded to her father, just so he was placated with an answer of some kind before she hurried away.

"Anyway, I better go check how things are out in the city," she quickly came up with an excuse. It wasn't a great one, but he often sent her to check on his territory, so it worked well enough.

"Yes, yes," Vladimir nodded, "You do that. I have to work on my plans. Now that he's violated my space, I'll need to move the workshop somewhere more secret... And make some kind of space to keep difficult customers like him, so they don't escape in future..."

He was muttering away to himself now, planning things out, so Dariya could take her chance and slipped away.

It only took her a few moments to reach Antonin's hideout and she hurried inside. He only needed to glance up and see her grave expression to know something was very wrong.

He jumped up off the floor and hurried over to her, "What? What is it?!" he demanded to know.

"My father knows more than he should. I think someone very powerful is working with him!" she got straight to the point.

He bit his lip, looking nervous, "How powerful?" he questioned.

"The Chief of Police..." she admitted to her suspicions.

Antonin lapsed into shocked silence as he considered Dariya's suggestion and its terrifying implications. They had given all their evidence to Sunnikov. She had been the one to bring him here...

So, surely, she couldn't be spying for Vladimir Volkov? He would have known more, and much sooner. But then again, how *had* Vladimir found him out? Sunnikov had been the only person in Yaroslavl's police force who had known his true identity...

Dariya must be right! How hadn't he realised this before? He had been so stupid and reckless, in his desperation to solve the case. He had forgotten about his own safety.

Now the case was bound to be compromised. Sunnikov would have all the information and evidence. Every blasted file. She could destroy it all!

He visibly paled. "You're serious? Th... I have to get out of here!" he looked around in a panic, checking for anything he might need to take with him.

"Get out of here? Why? You're still safe..."

"This isn't about me! She'll destroy the evidence! I have to go to someone higher up! If I go home, Ilya will help me, I'm sure." he explained.

"Ilya?"

"The Chief in Moscow. He sent me here at her request, but that was probably some kind of trap, so she could get rid of any evidence against your father, then pass the blame to another department. But if I speak to him before she can, then he'll know how to stop her. I can't, obviously, she outranks me..." he reasoned.

"How are you going to get to Moscow before she can do anything? She's had the evidence for days now. You still have to travel one hundred and seventy-three miles without getting murdered by my crazy family!" Dariya seemed flustered by the idea.

Antonin looked determined. "We'll just have to get there as quickly as we can. It's not like I have a choice. I can't let her do this."

"We?" Dariya frowned, confused by his sudden use of the plural pronoun.

"Well, I can't leave you here! You'll be in danger. Doesn't she know that you helped me?" he insisted.

She shook her head, "I told her everything I had to, but I kept my disguise on and I didn't tell her my name..."

"But she told me to target you because they suspected you would help me," he revealed, still concerned about her.

She shrugged, "They can't prove anything, and I know how to play my father by now. I'll get away with it. Besides, if we both vanish, it'll be more suspicious, and they'll definitely come after us. This way, they'll come after you and I'll try to distract and disrupt as much as I can."

He nodded, "I see..." he felt a little sad about that. He had hoped he could help her out of her, away from her insane family, before everything got a whole lot worse. But he had to focus on his mission.

"Then I'll appreciate any help you can give me. Best to get ready to go now..." he replied, knowing that he would have to be ready to leave. His only chance to save this case was to move faster than Sunnikov.

ESCAPING YAROSLAVL

Antonin left when darkness fell that evening, hoping that the night would provide him with some cover so that he wouldn't be spotted.

Again, Dariya came to his assistance. She waited until the search had stopped for the day and all of her siblings had returned home, then threw as much of Antonin's stuff as she could, as well as one or two other items she hoped would help him, into a big bag and slipped out of the house.

She had hoped using one of her own bags rather than his would avert suspicion, but she needn't have worried. The others seemed distracted. They were 'making progress reports' to her father, which seemed to consist of arguing over who had got closest to finding Antonin.

Knowing them, this argument would keep them occupied until Vladimir got bored and told them to shut up. He enjoyed watching his children squabble for his attention, so she probably had at least an hour.

She pulled a hood over her head as she left the house, trying to cover her face as much as she could. She never knew where her father's spies were these days. He was expanding his powerbase, intimidating or bribing people into reporting everything that happened in the city directly to him.

She had to be careful. So, she stuck to the shadows and walked quickly, heading down to the hotel where Antonin had briefly stayed. The car was parked at the roadside outside. She stopped by it and glanced around. No one seemed to be watching. She took his keys from her pocket and let herself into the vehicle, dumping the bag in the passenger seat.

Soon, she pulled up outside the warehouse-cum-hideout and honked the horn three times.

Antonin had been waiting for this. They had planned out his departure carefully, to try and minimise the danger. After all, the entire mission depended on him making it back to Moscow, alive and on time. They were both pinning their hopes on this.

He hurried out of the building and met her at the driver's door, ready to swap places and leave.

She climbed out and pulled her hood down to face him, fighting tears. Here was her first real friend, a man more like a brother to her than any of her real brothers had ever been. And she had to say goodbye and leave his fate in the hands of God because he had risked his life to help her.

She felt she should say something and searched for words that wouldn't make her cry. "I... I got as much of your stuff as I could. Sorry if I missed anything," she focused on the practicalities, the packing and preparing, because, as her father had always taught her, her emotions made her weak.

She had never considered him so stupid as she did now.

Antonin seemed upset too, "You did everything you could," he told her, his voice wobbling slightly. She got the impression he was talking about far more than the packing.

She nodded, "Right, I did. I added some stuff too. Things I think might help you if they come after you."

"And those are?" he was curious now, welcoming a distraction from their goodbyes, as well as any help he could get.

"You have a few knock-out grenades, an x-ray gun that should show you if anyone's hiding nearby, waiting to hurt you, and a radar that's on the frequency we use, so you can hear your pursuers talking to one another. They're at the top of the bag. Please use them if you need them!" she explained, hoping he would take her help. It would at least give her a little more peace of mind.

Antonin nodded solemnly, recognising what she had done just to try and keep him safe. Stealing from her father to help him was a grave risk. *Being here* with him was enough of a risk. But she hadn't hidden away from the danger.

He risked a small smile as he stooped to plant a chaste kiss on her cheek, "Thank you. For everything. I'll stay safe, I promise."

This time, Dariya gave in and let her tears fall as she stepped aside to let him leave, "Good luck then," Was her final goodbye.

He got into the car and shut the door, winding the window down and calling to her, "I could say the same to you. Stay safe."

With that, he pulled away and slammed his foot to the floor, determined to be out of Yaroslavl before the Volkovs came looking for him again.

This was, after all, his one chance to make his escape, and so he finally got to use the 'getaway' car's potential power.

Dariya watched until the car disappeared around a bend at the end of the road, then dried her eyes, pulled her hood up again, and walked away. She wanted to get home again before she was missed.

The journey was short and soon, she stepped back through the front door. The familiar sound of arguing already attacked her. Her siblings were still fighting it out in the living room. Ignoring their raised voices, she headed for the stairs. Time alone, hidden in her bedroom, was what she needed right now.

But as she got her foot to the bottom step, she heard the house phone ringing loudly. She hesitated. The only people who usually called the house were Vladimir's spies. At the moment, he was focusing his intelligence resources on hunting down Antonin.

That information alone told her she should wait and try to listen in, in case she could learn something about her friend's safety. Quietly, she snuck off the staircase and to the door, standing behind it tensely as she strained to hear.

The first sound was her father's voice, raised over the ringtone, "Shut up, everyone! This could be important!" then the phone abruptly seized its ringing as he snatched it up.

"Yes? Who is it?!"

There was silence now and Dariya silently cursed. Why couldn't he be using speakerphone or something? Of course, that would be too easy...

"I see." she heard him speak up again after a while, sounding grave.

A clicking sound followed and she guessed that he had put the phone down. Well, that was short and to the point. But then her father didn't waste time with small talk when it came to the important stuff. All he wanted was his information.

She was about to leave when she heard him speak again, this time in anger.

"You've all failed!" he yelled at his children, "That little rat has got away from us! His car is gone!"

How on Earth had someone noticed so quickly? She had been careful, she had checked, no one had watched her, she was sure of that... He really *must* have agents everywhere, who had been checking up on the car regularly. In which case, she had been lucky *not* to have been seen.

It was bad news for Antonin though. The sooner her father knew he had escaped from Yaroslavl, the sooner the chase would begin.

"What are you fools staring at? Get out there and find him!" She heard her father roar. It was already beginning.

DMITRI AND
THE CHASE

Perhaps he was paranoid, but Antonin kept glancing in his mirror to see if anyone was behind him for any length of time as he sped back to Moscow.

Most of the time, there wasn't anyone close to him. He wasn't too surprised by that. He was technically speeding, after all. But it was an emergency, he reasoned to himself.

No sooner had he thought that than he looked back and noticed a familiar car pulling into the gap behind him. His blood ran cold. It was the Volkovs' car, the very same that Dariya had rescued him in. But he could already tell that it wasn't her driving.

He slammed his foot to the floor, pushing his car even harder, but his pursuer kept up with him determinedly. Cursing, he tried to think. He had to get rid of them somehow because he still had over a hundred miles to go and they were right on his tail.

Out of the corner of his eye, he saw movement in his mirror. Looking back, he spotted someone leaning out of the passenger's window of the chasing car. It was a man with a gun. He was trying to aim it towards Antonin's back window.

Somehow, he doubted this was just an idle threat.

His heart was in his mouth now, but still, he waited. He had thought of a plan now, but he had to wait until the right moment if he wanted to avoid the bullet. Swerving sharply across the road, he heard the gun fire behind him. This time, he didn't dare look back, he simply prayed that he had timed his dodge correctly.

Someone shouted obscenities from behind him at about the same time as a stray bullet whizzed by. He had been lucky this time.

He knew, though, that it wouldn't be the last shot, and that dodging like that was a dangerous game to keep playing. He was going to need another play if he was going to make it back to Moscow.

He thought of the presents Dariya had brought him. Would they help him at a time like this? He knew there was someone behind him, he didn't need help figuring that out and he doubted they were bothering with radio communication at a time like this. That left the possibility of stunning them.

It was risky, on a public road. If it worked, it would cause a crash. But if it failed, he wasn't likely to survive.

Still steering with one hand, driving erratically now, he unzipped his bag and reached inside, groping in the dark to try and find a knock-out grenade without taking his eyes off the road ahead.

His hand grabbed onto something and he pulled it out, taking a quick glance down to confirm his suspicions. He had the grenade ready.

He fumbled with the window, opening it just in time to hear

another bullet whizz by. That sound made him feel giddy with excitement and nerves. He was in the heart of a deadly situation now. Would he last long enough to throw his grenade, the only weapon he had, his only hope of getting back to Moscow alive?

Dariya lay on her bed in silence, listening to her own depressing thoughts. She knew two of her siblings had taken the car and some weapons. They had gone after Antonin.

Even if he had been going hell for leather, there was no way he would have got very far before they had left.

They had his car's registration plate memorised and were horribly determined to hunt him down.

So, there would be a chase and sooner or later, there would be a fight. It would be a fight to the death at this point because there was no room for discussion with killing machines, which was what most of her siblings had been raised to be.

And all she could do was lay and pray that Antonin would somehow come out on top, even though he was up against two heavily armed, half-crazed killers and he was one man, armed with nothing remotely deadly and too given to compassion for a ruthless showdown.

She knew what all this added up to: Her only friend would die. Her cruel blood relatives would kill the kindest family member she had ever had.

And, with no transportation and no allies, she had no way to save him.

Tears welled up in her eyes and she lay there numbly, making no effort to dry them. They poured over her cheeks as she began to weep. She wept for Antonin first, then for his family.

In this, she included the fiancée he had spoken of, a woman who would have dreamt of a wedding, only to have it snatched from her. She included herself too, someone who had become so close to him in such a short space of time but would never see him again now. There was no one else. He hadn't mentioned any real family.

Then she found she was crying more for herself because she had messed everything up. She had begged him, selfishly, to give her a better life. True, he might have intervened because of his job, even if she hadn't been there, but what she should have done was stop him from doing that by scaring him away somehow.

She hadn't, though, because she hadn't been able to face being a prisoner in her father's city, forced to go along with his twisted regime, forever.

So, she had first betrayed her family, as her father would put it. This was apparently the worst of crimes. Then she had lured a young man to his death. That was something she felt far worse about.

Even her attempt to help him had been wrong. She thought she was helping him when she turned over the evidence, but she had helped her father's spy instead.

And now her friend was gone. So was her chance to get out of here.

Now she was crying hard, practically sobbing. In her current state, she didn't fully realise that until Dmitri stuck his head around the door and stared at her.

"You okay there, Sis? I heard you crying..."

She tensed. This meant trouble. If her family noticed, they would start asking questions and wouldn't accept her answers unless they were suitably awkward for her. After all, they had been raised not to believe in emotions and to treat everyone with suspicion. Apart from Papa Dearest, who was clearly an angel.

She stopped herself there. Why was she thinking like this? With most of her family members, cynicism and bitterness were normal and justified, but this was Dmitri, her cheerful, sweet little brother. He somehow seemed to have resisted this lesson and remained innocent, just wanting to help his whole family.

The others looked down on him for that. But he didn't mind. He just trusted his family's judgement.

Through her sadness, an idea snuck. She sat up, "Come in and shut the door."

Antonin took a deep breath and threw the grenade out of his window, hoping to at least get it close enough to the car behind to knock the shooter and their driver unconscious. Hopefully, if their window was still open, it would be possible for the knock-out gas to be released into the car.

The grenade spun from his grip and into the road, landing with a crack. He cursed. It had missed the car. They'd probably not be affected now.

But, to his surprise and relief, the driver rode straight over the grenade and a piece of the metal casing snapped off, sinking into their tyre with a loud BANG!

The car veered off the road, out of control from the sudden loss of a tyre at such a high speed.

He stopped looking after that. It was enough that they were off his tail. He didn't want to hang about and see if they survived or not.

Instead, he urged his vehicle on. The rest of the journey, though long, seemed to speed by peacefully, now that he was free from the attacks of the Volkovs.

Soon, he was driving past the Moscow signs and he breathed out, sighing in relief. It was okay, he had made it home.

Everything might just be alright after all.

BIG NEWS

Antonin drove into the familiar car park at the Moscow police station, stopped the car and took a moment to relax. It was finally over.

Then he sprang into action again. The nightmare trip might be over, and he may be out of immediate danger, but the mission wasn't over yet. He had to find Ilya and expose Sunnikov.

Jumping out of the car, he hurried inside, barging past colleagues, ignoring them as they called out to him. He felt a little bad, but he didn't have time for small talk yet. Later, he would catch up with everyone. Now, he needed Ilya's help.

He strode down the corridor to the Chief's office and shoved his way inside. He wouldn't normally barge in on Ilya like this, but time wasn't on his side and he had to expose Sunnikov before she could destroy his carefully gathered evidence.

Ilya looked up from his paperwork with a grim expression and gasped. "Antonin! What are you doing here?!" he seemed confused.

That's right, Antonin remembered suddenly, his return wasn't 'official'. Ilya hadn't been expecting him.

But he didn't have time to notify him, and he certainly didn't have time to explain everything right now, "I need your help!" he blurted out.

"What with?" Ilya's confusion was only growing worse as Antonin spoke.

The younger man pulled the door shut behind him. He couldn't be too careful. Then he finally began to explain how his trip had gone and why he needed Ilya's help.

His boss simply sat and listened, open-mouthed. He had expected a complicated case, but nothing like this. What could he do? If everything Antonin was telling him was true, he would have to start a federal investigation...

The key was if it was true. He'd have to prove it if there was going to be that kind of investigation. "That all sounds... Insane, frankly. But do you have any proof?"

"Of the part with the Volkovs, yes. Well, I did. I handed it over to Sunnikov and only realised she must be spying later. But I don't have any proof that she is..." Antonin sighed as he trailed off.

This was it, then. Even Ilya wouldn't believe him, or if he did, he couldn't do anything. They had lost, after all this. He had fought so hard just to be here, and it had all been for nothing.

Ilya paused for thought. There might not be much he could do, without proof, but he trusted Antonin's word on this. Besides, the man was clearly distressed, something was wrong.

Perhaps he could encourage an investigation without actually accusing her... The idea made him smile and he turned to Antonin to share the good news.

"Well, I can't accuse her of misconduct without evidence, but I can suggest a review of her department. After all, if she got us involved, she obviously doesn't trust her own team, so she should have opened a review anyway. But I'm guessing she wanted to shift blame, not draw attention to herself. I didn't suggest a review sooner because she was an old friend, but it might be necessary after all." he explained, considering the facts as he spoke.

Antonin still looked unconvinced, "Will that be quick enough? She could still get rid of the evidence..."

"The department's activities will be frozen under review and she'll be being watched. I doubt she'll be able to get rid of the evidence in those circumstances," Ilya told him calmly. "Which will mean that the reviewers will learn about the case and it'll be suspicious if anything should happen afterwards."

"And you can definitely make this happen?" Antonin sought further reassurance, not wanting to fail at this crucial stage.

"Of course I can. You leave it to me," Ilya assured him with a great deal more confidence than he actually had.

He could tell Antonin wouldn't stop worrying unless he convinced him, but it wasn't up to him. It depended on whether he could persuade the regulating bodies an investigation was necessary. And persuade them in time.

Dariya waited until Dmitri had followed her instructions and shut the door, leaving the two of them alone, then spoke to him.

"Can you keep a secret for me, Dima?"

"Sure," he shrugged, not seeing the importance of this.

She gave him a hard stare. She couldn't gamble with this if he wasn't going to take it seriously. "I mean it. You can't tell *anyone.*"

"No one at all?" he checked.

"No one." she shook her head firmly.

He considered this in silence for a moment or two. Dariya was a little bit surprised by that. She hadn't expected her happy-go-lucky little brother to give it much thought. Perhaps she had underestimated him.

That could be a good thing or a terrible thing, depending on his response. She waited, without much patience.

After a while, his answer came as he nodded slowly, "Alright, I'll keep it a secret for you. What is it?"

"I'm worried about Antonin," she began to confide in him.

"After everything he did to you?" he wrinkled his brow in confusion, and she sighed. He had fallen for their father's lies. He had told endless tales of Antonin being evil.

"He didn't do anything to me. He tried to help me!" she told him. It might be a mistake to pour her heart out like this, but she wasn't sure she could keep quiet anymore. Hiding from her family all the time was becoming a strain. Besides, Dmitri was harmless.

She began to explain the truth about her and Antonin to him, backtracking to the start, when they had first met, and explaining everything.

He listened attentively and finally spoke up when she stopped, "I see... So, you wanted to run away from home?" he sounded sad now and she felt a stab of guilt.

"Not home as much as Papa," she admitted.

He fell silent again, before finally muttering, "So I'm not the only one... I've always felt he was the reason why... Why the others bully me, you know," she heard him sniffle and felt worse.

Dmitri always seemed so happy, but she had reduced him to sadness now. Or perhaps he had always been sad, secretly. He had just hidden behind smiles.

She put her arms around him, "I know... I'm sorry I can't do anything."

"It's not your fault... It's always so hopeless here," he murmured as he rested against her.

"That's why I wanted to leave. But then I saw things differently. I thought Antonin could help... But now he's gone, and I can't do anything to protect him." she revealed her thoughts to him.

He looked up at her again and managed to smile through his tears, "Maybe he can help, if we find him again and protect him."

That was what she had hoped too. Maybe her plan would work. "I'm not sure I can go... Papa would notice." she bit her lip, nervous and guilty.

Pushing him to go was cruel. It put him in terrible danger. But he wouldn't be noticed as much, so he was her only chance to get away with this. He seemed to follow her thoughts, reading between the lines in a way that made her question his 'dumb' act again.

"But he wouldn't notice if I went. I can get a train to Moscow and try to find him before the others do."

"And you'll do that? Even though it's dangerous?" she asked him hopefully.

"It's not like I have anything better to do," he admitted, "This way, at least I can try and do some good!" he cheered up a bit.

She returned his smile, trying to cheer up herself, as she helped him get ready to go. No one noticed him slip away from the house, no one questioned it.

Antonin was also oblivious to the help Dariya was sending his way. He had found something far more important to do. And, for once in a while, it wasn't related to his case.

No, now he had been assured that he could leave that in Ilya's hands, he had something else on his mind.

Nikolina.

He grabbed his stuff from the car and hurried back to her house, letting himself in. It was very quiet inside, there didn't seem to be anyone about downstairs, so he went up to her room to look for her.

Peering around the door, he spotted her, sat on the bed with her back to him. She appeared to be engrossed in writing. Well, that was typical. She always was a bit of a workaholic.

He smiled fondly, then decided to let her know he was back. It was about time, after all. It had been too long since he had seen her.

"Lina?" he called to her.

She dropped her notebook and jumped up, whirling around to face him in one swift moment. "Antonin!!" she ran over to him and threw her arms around him enthusiastically.

He caught her in his arms, laughing, "Miss me that much?"

"Of course!"

"I missed you too, babe! But look, I'm back. Didn't I tell you I'd get back alright?" he was so relieved to be back and holding again that he couldn't help but gloat.

"You did. But that is not the point. The point is that you are home, safe and sound. Now we can start planning our wedding, right?" she suggested.

Antonin nodded, "We definitely need to work on that. But let's catch up first, while I unpack," he suggested, finally, reluctantly pulling away from her and turning to the huge bag that he had dumped in the doorway.

"That is not the bag you left with," she pointed out.

"I know. I got into some trouble and a friend helped me out. It's her bag," he explained.

"That was good of her. What trouble were you in?" she pressed.

He sighed. She wasn't going to like the explanation, but equally, she wouldn't stop asking until she had heard it.

"It's a long story, Lina, I'll explain later, okay? I don't want to have to repeat it for everyone. Where *is* everyone, anyway? Quietest it's been here for ages..." he changed the subject.

"Oh, well, Papa is at work, of course, and so is Sasha. He got another case, so he is enjoying work again, thank goodness. I think Katya is at college, but with her, you never know," she explained.

He nodded. That made sense. Everything seemed normal here. And after the week he had had, that was a welcome relief.

"And what about your work? How did your case go?" he continued to question her as he opened his bag and began to pull out the devices Dariya had given him.

"I won!" she smiled, "I have had a few cases since, as well. It is going pretty we-- What on Earth are those?!" she stopped in her tracks, staring at the things he was holding.

"Oh, that's great!" he smiled back at her, then followed her gaze to what he was holding.

Currently, it was one of the x-ray devices Dariya had given him. "Oh, this is something my friend gave me to help on my mission," he explained, "Let me show you..." he pointed it at her, ignoring her startled expression as he pulled the trigger.

She was about to demand an explanation when he turned the display screen so they could both see. "Then it shows an x-ray, se---" he cut himself off, having spotted something.

Nikolina was staring at the screen too. She turned to him in shock as she saw what he had seen. Then they were suddenly hugging again, emotional.

This was turning out to be Antonin's best day for a while, though he really hadn't expected to learn he was going to be a father from one of Vladimir Volkov's weird toys.

Things at the Volkov house weren't quite so cheerful and they were certainly having a harder time forgetting about Antonin's mission.

The two Volkov agents who had failed to catch him had, after a long trapse at the side of the road, arguing all the way, returned home with nothing more to show for their mission than a few minor injuries.

As a result, a furious Vladimir had called another 'emergency meeting' to rant about 'the Antonin problem', as he called it.

Dariya was there, standing at the back reluctantly and hoping no one noticed Dmitri's absence. She still had her fingers crossed that everything was going well for him. The return of her very annoyed and mildly injured siblings had been a relief, but what else was going on in his life right now? It surely wouldn't be that simple to escape her obsessive, vengeful father...

Her father was talking, "Right, since we didn't catch him while he was on the run, we'll need to track him down. Vadim? I asked you to do some research on him. Don't you let me down as well."

The young man in question shook his head nervously, "No, I found some stuff! I got his phone number and an address. It's not his though. Apparently, he lives with his girlfriend."

Someone interrupted at this point, confused. "I thought Dariya was his girlfriend?"

Vladimir took over again now, having found another reason to hate Antonin, "Clearly, the slimy little rat was two-timing her! And this little 'girlfriend' was probably in on it... What do you know about her?!"

Dariya flinched. He had found another innocent person to drag into it. Now Antonin's fiancée was a target too.

Vadim started talking again, "Her name's Nikolina Moroz. Apparently, she's the Moscow Police Chief's daughter..."

"Great, another damn cop! Put Moroz and his family on the

hitlist too, would you?"

Dariya tuned out at this point, mostly due to panic. What could she do now? A whole family were in danger because of her! She had to find a way to warn them before anything happened.

She couldn't use Dmitri this time. He had already left. Besides, he was just protection, he wasn't meant to get directly involved with Antonin and his family. That would be too risky. If he got discovered, their father wouldn't hesitate to cut him down as well.

But now her father was talking about sending some more killers to Moscow to take these people out and while they would be slowed down by train travel - Since the car had been the major casualty of Antonin's escape - They would find their targets unsuspecting and unarmed.

She had to do something. The only option was to contact Antonin directly. She elbowed a sister aside and slipped through the crowd of siblings until she was standing behind Vadim, able to see the phone number scrawled on his notebook.

It was time to take some direct action again before an innocent family were murdered.

THE CALL AND
THE WEDDING

The phone ringing interrupted Antonin's attempt to catch up with his girlfriend. He sighed and reluctantly pulled away from her.

"I better answer that," he said.

Nikolina nodded, "I guess so," she did her best to understand. He was busy. But she had missed him so much, lying awake worrying about him at night. Now he was home, safe, and to top it all off, she had just learnt that she was carrying his baby.

Yet still, they couldn't spend any time together. She tried not to mind too much though because work was important to her and she knew his job was important to him too.

So, she sat there and waited for his attention to come back to her, putting her hand to her stomach as she waited. The news had been sudden and hard to process, but of course, it was a good thing. They would finally have a family of their own...

While his girlfriend was deep in thought, Antonin picked up the phone and hesitated. He didn't know who was calling or what to say.

He didn't get a chance to speak as Dariya's voice piped up as soon as he answered, coming across quickly and panicked.

"It's me, Dariya. Sorry, I don't have time to explain how I got this number or time to talk. I just hope you're there and you got home safely. But you're in danger again, you, your girlfriend and her whole family too. All of you need to get out of there! Go into hiding or something, change your names, whatever you need to do!"

For a moment, he was completely overwhelmed. Then he shook his head disbelievingly. No, they couldn't be in danger, not now. All that was behind him. Ilya was tying up the loose ends of the case and then he and Nikolina would move on to live happily ever after.

After all, after such a happy day, how could he believe otherwise?

"Dariya, calm down. I'm sure it's not that bad," he tried to assure her.

"Not that bad? Please, listen to me! They've found your address and some people are coming to kill you, her and anyone else they can find!" she practically yelled at him.

He froze up. Suddenly, it all seemed real again. He could picture the Volkovs bursting into the house with guns. Nikolina's face rose up in his mind. He couldn't let them do this to her.

"I... I see. Thank you for letting me know. I have to do something, fast! My fiancée did nothing to them, I can't let them kill her and our child!" he thought aloud as he tried to come up with a plan.

"She's pregnant?!" Dariya's surprise was evident.

"Yeah. We just found out," he told her.

"Damn... On any other occasion, I'd offer you my congratulations, but right now all I can say is keep your family safe. I've sent what help I can, but I don't know if it'll be enough."

"We'll have to see what we can do," Antonin agreed, "Don't worry, I'll think of something," Was his last reassurance before he hung up. He had planning to do.

Well, his top priority was Nikolina. Not only was she the love of his life, but she was carrying his child. He had to protect her.

He also had to make good his promise to her. Yes, that should be the first thing, to marry her. Then if they killed him, he would at least die knowing he had fulfilled his promise. And she would be taken care of as a widow, allowing her to provide for their child.

But he probably didn't have much time to do this. The wedding plans would have to be dispensed with and it would have to be done as quickly as possible instead.

On the other hand, that wouldn't be that difficult. Nikolina was on good terms with the local priest, and he would probably agree to do a ceremony. They'd just need a witness.

That meant involving someone else at short notice. Where was he going to find someone to drag in?

Ekaterina sauntered into the house casually and waved at him, "Hey, you're back and you didn't die, nice going!"

"Thanks. What are you doing this afternoon?" he got straight to the point.

She gave him an odd look, "Why? You better not be trying to two-time my sister!"

He laughed, "No, no. I need someone to come to our wedding."

"That's today? Damn, you two move *fast*. Sure," she shrugged.

And that was why she was the perfect person to ask. She wouldn't ask awkward questions.

Nikolina, on the other hand, might be harder to persuade. So, he settled for just sticking his head around the bedroom door and calling, "Hey, Lina, call that priest guy you know, will you? We're getting married this afternoon!" then running off before she could question it

He had somehow managed to play that off a lot more casually than he had expected, given that he felt like screaming the whole time. There were a few more things he had to plan for, of course, he had to make sure Ilya sent someone to handle the case and he wanted to leave something behind for his child, in case something happened to him.

There was also the matter of Dariya and what would become of her if the case against her father failed. He was worried about her, but he wasn't sure how to help her.

He would have to put together a to-do list of things to handle after the wedding. Get married, make sure everything and everyone important was taken care of... Then it would be fine to go on the run if he had to, without worrying that he was abandoning anyone.

That seemed like the best way to distract them and lure them away from his family, after all. The other option was taking them with him and there was no safe way to do that. No, he would have to run for it.

And if going on the run wasn't enough to throw the Volkovs off the scent... At least he would die knowing he had done what he could to protect the family.

These thoughts were still running through his mind that afternoon when he met Katya and Nikolina at the church. Somehow, despite the short notice and her obvious confusion, Nikolina had acquired herself a white dress. Katya had also dressed up.

Antonin hadn't bothered too much. His shirt was clean, and he had put a tie on, but he hadn't had time to acquire a full suit. This would have to do.

Still avoiding his bride's questions, he made his way into the church and tried to hold back tears as he said his vows. Putting into words what Nikolina meant to him somehow made the threat of losing her so much more real.

He heard Katya making 'eww' sounds in the background, the priest tutting at her and a camera clicking as the church's resident photographer for such occasions took a picture, but he wasn't thinking about any of that. He just pulled his new wife into his arms and held on tight, knowing this might be the last time he held her.

PREPARATION

The night after the wedding, Antonin didn't sleep much. This wasn't because he was enjoying his honeymoon, either. Instead, he sat up in Ilya's living room, trying to take care of everything he needed to do. He didn't know how much time he had.

He wasn't sure where to start though. He had opened a notebook but couldn't think of a word to write. If he died, what might the ones he had left behind need to know?

There was only one person he could think of to ask for advice at a time like this. He just hoped she would be able to answer, that she wasn't asleep or with someone she couldn't talk around.

He dialled the number Dariya had called him from before and waited as it rang.

"Hello?" her voice spoke to him tentatively through the darkness.

"Can you talk?" he asked, double-checking before he told her anything important.

"Of course," she confirmed.

"Well... I need some advice. If... If anything should happen, what do my family need to know to stay safe?"

She didn't answer for a moment, "I hope it doesn't come to this, but..." there was another moment of silence and he tensed, wondering what she would say, "Tell them about me and how to find me. I'll help them."

Antonin was confused now, "Won't coming to you put them *and* you in danger?"

"Perhaps it will, but I didn't help you as much as I could have done because I was afraid to stand up to my father. But now... He's pushing me too far. I'm going to raise a rebellion against him. Any loved one of yours who ever needs my help will find it, I promise you. And if I fail, I'll leave them a diary or something to explain everything," she told him, suddenly full of strength and fire.

Her words worried him a little. It was hard to picture sweet, kind Dariya leading an army. And it was bound to put her life on the life.

"Rebellion? What are you talking about?"

"He says it's time I had children, again. And he's going to try some weird age acceleration on them, so they'll be 'useful' sooner. Well, if he's going to weaponise my children, I'll come right back at him and raise them to hate his gates. A whole new generation can easily overthrow him," she explained.

He could hear the bitterness in her tone. It made him nervous. It wasn't like the soft, kind Dariya he had known. He was beginning to suspect that somewhere beneath that persona lurked a warrior. Vladimir didn't know what he had got himself in for when he had screwed up his daughter.

"Well... I wish you luck with that. And you'll be there for my family if anything happens?" he steered the conversation back to his original point.

"Absolutely. But warn them: Don't trust my father. He'll try and trick them," she told him.

He nodded, "Thanks for the heads-up. I can give them a little more preparation now..." then he lingered. The conversation had reached its natural end but now neither of them wanted to go.

Eventually, she sighed, "It's late. I should go... I miss you."

"I miss you too. Stay safe," he replied.

She didn't answer, she didn't return that comment. She couldn't because she knew he wasn't going to be safe. She hung up the phone and lay on her bed, not sleeping.

Antonin put his phone down and began to write carefully. The first thing he felt he had to do was to write something for his child. If he died, he would never get to meet them. They deserved to know why that was, but he knew if something happened to him, Nikolina would be too heartbroken to explain things properly, even if she figured them out for herself.

Which was why he hadn't told her about the danger he was in yet. She had worried enough last time when he had left for his mission. He didn't want her to go back to worrying again as soon as he had got back. No, he would tell her another time.

But when it came to his child, he would feel guilty not addressing the issue personally. Nikolina had had time with him, she had memories and he hoped they would have more time together. His child had nothing, and if he couldn't return, they would never know the truth.

But if the diary was found... Then they would be in danger. He had to be careful here, in case, if the worst-case scenario occurred, he was dead and the Volkovs were in control.

Dariya had promised her help, though. He didn't like to do this. It felt like he was incriminating her, but she would be the best person to guide his child through something difficult like this.

He wrote out a message with her address, just to be sure.

Now what? Nikolina... Would Nikolina get involved? He had a feeling she would hide away. That was her usual response to things that upset her. She never spoke of her mother's death, for example.

That was why he worried their child wouldn't get any support from her and would need Dariya's help.

Would she give the child the diary though? He hadn't thought of that problem and now, it bothered him. He would have to find someone who would. Ekaterina, possibly. She didn't know the truth, but she had helped him without question before, and unlike her other relatives, she wouldn't be intrigued enough to look inside, so she would probably the safest person to entrust it to.

Still, though, it hurt him too much to consider not leaving Nikolina something to remember him by. Perhaps he should leave her something special, and a little carefully hidden advice as well, just in case she took things differently than he expected. Just in case she decided to get revenge upon the Volkovs.

He knew how to do that. It would fulfil another promise. When he had started dabbling in music, he had promised to write her a love song. Now, he could leave it for her and if he managed to get out of this situation alive, he would sing it for her one day. If not, he would leave a secret message encoded in the music. He was sure he could do that if he thought about it. It would be safe from prying eyes, and this way, even in her grief, she would be sure to keep it. A note, she would throw away, but not a gift.

He sat up the rest of the night, writing until he had got the perfect song to express his feelings, as well as acting Dariya's advice to warn her about Vladimir.

In the early hours of the morning, he scribbled another note and slipped it, with the diary, under Ekaterina's door. He could only hope she would keep it to herself.

Now he was ready. He wouldn't be leaving any loose ends if anything happened to him now. All he had to do was wait for the Volkovs to attack, so he could lure them away from his unsuspecting family.

THE VOLKOVS
INVADE

The attack began a little while before dawn. Antonin had sat up, lying in wait. He didn't want to be unprepared. Thankfully, everyone else was asleep, out of harm's way.

The house had been silent all night and it was beginning to get to him as he sat at the living room table tensely, but eventually, the silence was broken by the twinkling sound of shattering glass. They had broken the kitchen window, he guessed, focusing on where the sound had come from. He jumped up and ran to the kitchen, checking his pocket for knock-out grenades as he did so. There were only two left. He had to be careful now. They were the only serious weapon he had on him. No doubt his attackers were much better equipped.

Even after that thought, he headed towards the danger because it was better to face them than let them sneak up on him, or worse, sneak up on his family. He was just outside the kitchen door when he froze. He could hear them talking. Perhaps if he listened, they would say something that might give him an idea of their plan.

"Right, so we're looking for Jelennski... And there's some girl?" Someone checked in a rather confused voice.

"Yes!" A fed-up voice responded, "But we might as well just get rid of everyone here. There's some other copper here as well," she explained.

"So, where are they?" the first voice asked.

"They're not going to be awake right now, are they? Let's go upstairs..."

Antonin cursed internally. He hadn't heard anything useful and now they were heading this way. He'd have to engage them now to stop them getting to the stairs.

He stepped into the doorway. "What the hell do you think you're doing?!" he demanded to know, hoping to stop them in their tracks.

The two men exchanged glances, then one of them hissed to the other, "That's him, get him!"

The bigger man rushed at him, while the second moved his hand down to his belt as if to pull out a weapon.

Now Antonin didn't keep his curses in his head, swearing loudly as he turned and broke into a run, sprinting through the house. He heard footsteps behind him and hoped they were both following him. Dangerous as that was, if one of them stayed behind then his plan had failed.

Then a gunshot rang through the night.

He ducked down, sliding beneath the living room table as the bullet whizzed over it. Standing up on the other side, he saw it stuck in the wall at exactly the right height to have hit the back of his head. He was lucky he had fast reactions.

Running towards the door, he thought he heard someone move upstairs and prayed his pursuers hadn't heard anything as he grabbed the door handle and pulled it open, dashing out into the night.

It wasn't until he reached the corner of the street that he dared to glance back and saw them both running at him. Now there wasn't just one gun pointing at him.

Well... Wasn't this what he had wanted? He had got them away from the house and he was certainly getting an 'adventure' fleeing from them. He just wished he had a proper weapon and that he had hung onto his getaway car.

But he hadn't, so he was just going to have to rely on fast running and dumb luck. Which didn't give him great chances against two angry, armed mobsters. It was pretty desperate situation, but he had to hope he was quicker and smarter than them. Otherwise, he was dead.

Nikolina lay completely still in her bed for a few minutes, trying to decide if she had heard anything or not. It could have been a dream...

But there was still something, some background sound she couldn't quite place running through the house. Perhaps it was just someone moving about. Antonin hadn't come to bed yet, after all. She had wondered about that. He hadn't seemed himself today. It had been a happy occasion, of course, but her usually bubbly husband had been distant.

It made her question if she had done something to upset him, somehow. But if that was the case, then why on Earth had he married her? He had been quite insistent that, instead of planning a beautiful wedding with their friends and families, they get married that afternoon in a sudden, secret ceremony.

And she had gone along with it, despite her dislike of spontaneity, because their relationship was more important to her than one day being perfectly planned. Then he seemed to be upset with her about something. She didn't understand any of this. Something wasn---

That time, there was definitely a noise. A sharp, sinister one, like a gun going off. It rang through the house.

She froze up. What should she do? What was happening? Her husband...

Was in danger. It came to her suddenly. How had she not seen this before? After everything he had told her about his mission, he had then started behaving strangely and now, something had happened to him.

Well, she wasn't going to lie here any longer and leave him like that! She jumped out of bed and ran. She charged into her father's room first, because she wanted to save Antonin, but if someone down there had a weapon, her father was more likely to be able to defend against them than she was. Even when panicking, she had to be practical.

Ilya was, unfortunately, a very deep sleeper though and she

charged into his room, only to have to shake him awake, uncomfortably conscious that while she was trying to rouse him, there was something else going on. A door slammed.

"Papa, wake up!!" she screamed at him in frustration, feeling her fear mounting. She needed his help *now!*

Ilya rolled over and squinted at her through half-open eyes, "Wha'?"

"Something's happening! Antonin's gone and I heard a gun and I don't know what's happening!!" she babbled.

And suddenly, he somehow seemed to be fully awake, pulling himself out of bed, "Alright, sweetheart, calm down. I'll check it out," he opened his bedside drawer and pulled out a taser.

She took a breath and tried to compose herself, "I... I'm going to come with you," she nodded after a moment.

He gave her a sharp look, which was slightly spoilt by the fact he was still in his pyjamas. "Are you sure that's wise? I don't want you in danger."

"My *husband* is in danger," she pointed out, equally sharp.

He sighed. She was a little *too* like him sometimes. "Very well, but still behind me," he commanded.

She didn't argue. That was why she had wanted him there. Because she wanted to save Antonin, but she didn't feel that brave on her own. He took the lead and headed downstairs, brandishing his taser in front of him. But everything was quiet now and no one was around.

"Well, darling, I think maybe--" Ilya was about to cast doubt on whether she had heard anything, after all, when he saw something embedded in the wall. A bullet.

He paled visibly and a concerned Nikolina followed his gaze. He heard her gasp and fought to reassure her, despite his own rising worry.

"Now, don't panic, dear. I'll... I'll call for back-up and we'll find out what's going on here..."

Nikolina paused again, pulling herself together and thinking as quickly as she could. Her jaw set determinedly, she nodded to him, "Right, you stay here and do that," she headed for the door.

"Where are you going?!" Ilya seemed startled that she would contemplate leaving in this kind of dangerous situation.

"To find my husband, of course," she answered coolly. She knew it was dangerous, she knew it was foolish, but right now, all that mattered was that she was there for him when she needed him. Even if it meant they would die together.

FIGHTING TO THE DEATH

Antonin kept running, though it was getting harder to breathe and he could hear his own heartbeat pounding through his head. It wasn't like he had a choice. He couldn't stop or he'd die.

The trouble was he wasn't sure how much longer he could keep running. It was getting harder and harder to keep going and the Volkovs were gaining on him.

He looked around for a way to escape, desperately hunting for anything that would give him the upper hand.

But he had dragged them out onto the edge of the city again, trying to avoid putting anyone else in danger. Here, there was nothing but sleepy suburban streets. No one else would suffer.

But he couldn't see how this would help *him*. Well, maybe he had run far enough now. He had got them away from any innocent bystanders, that was good enough. Besides, he couldn't go much further. He'd have to grab his grenades and take his chances. It might work, after all. And if not... Well, he wasn't afraid to die. He had made sure he didn't have any unfinished business. He could take the hit without feeling, in his final moments, that he had left regrets. Making peace with himself with that thought, he stopped running, ducking into an alleyway instead. It was a dead-end, but it was cover enough to keep him safe while he tried to find his weapons.

Closing his eyes, he slipped a hand into one pocket and drew out a grenade. Pulling out the pin, he threw it around the corner. Then he lay back against the wall, waiting for his pulse to calm down and things to go quiet before he checked to see if it had worked.

He heard a clatter, something rolling and then a splash. Then some shouting:

"Hey, what happened? Where did he go?!"

"He's in the alleyway, idiot. Didn't you see that? He's trying to attack us with grenades. Stupid guy can't throw right, but he rolled one down the gutter. It's the drain now, so that might blow up his precious city!" Someone snorted.

Damn! Antonin cursed in his head. How had he forgotten that the gutter was there, and the drain was open? Granted, it wouldn't blow up, it not being a proper grenade, but it meant he only had one weapon left and they knew where he was hiding.

He fumbled with the other one, trying to pull it out as their running footsteps hurtled towards him.

The two men skidded around the corner and both raised the guns at the same time. He was cornered, but the grenade was still in his hand.

He watched them carefully, trying to gauge whether or not he would get away with moving. The movement would be swift and brief, a second long - That was all it would take to throw the grenade.

But how quick were their reactions? Were they watching him as closely as he was watching them? Would he get away with it?

He didn't have a choice, so he pulled the pin back with one finger, under the cover of his sleeve. It was time to find out how lucky he was.

Ilya watched his daughter walk away with a growing sense of helplessness. He couldn't bring himself to stop her, though he knew she would be in danger if she followed him. He wanted to protect her, but he couldn't stop her from being with her husband in his hour of need, could he?

Besides, there was something more important he could do for Antonin. There was still the case against the Volkovs to attend to and he could take fingerprints from the broken window to prove that they were involved here. More evidence. Not that it would be of much use if he didn't get rid of Sunnikov. But now he had greater grounds to do so. The case wasn't just in her area anymore. It was a federal matter.

He waited for his team to arrive and take the fingerprints, ignoring their questioning looks. He knew they were all curious about this. Not just the fact that a crime had happened in his house, but where and how he lived in general. He kept things at work very professional, but now they had the chance to snoop.

He let them. He had bigger priorities. He had to push for that investigation now, even if it was ridiculously early in the morning. The situation had become urgent. He grabbed the phone and made some calls to some very powerful people.

The responses were generally disgruntled, due to the time, but changed very quickly when he explained the gravity of the situation.

It seemed as though they were ready to listen, after all. Sunnikov's downfall may be beginning.

Nikolina stepped out into the cold dark morning and looked around carefully. Where would Antonin have gone if he was under attack? She tried to think like him, and it came to her in a flash. Away from the city centre, into the suburbs. He wouldn't have wanted to put anyone in danger.

Was that what this had all been about? Keeping other people safe while he was at risk? It was very typical of him and very noble, but she couldn't help but feel it was stupid. He had put himself in danger. If he had just told her, she would have...

Done what? She could have told her father, who probably already knew since he had known about the mission in the first place. And he would have done what he was already doing - The best he could do if he followed all the rules. And right now, even with her own legalistic outlook, following the rules seemed stupid too. Someone was in danger!

She couldn't have done anything if he had told her. She wasn't sure she could do anything now. But she decided as she set off determinedly towards the nearest suburbs, she was going anyway because she had to try.

After a few yards, she thought of Antonin again and broke into a run. The sooner she reached him, the better she would feel. Even she couldn't do anything, she'd be there to reassure him. If they had to, they could run away together, somewhere where these Volkov people would never find them.

She was running through the suburban streets when she saw something fly from an alleyway. It whizzed over the wall on the opposite side of the road and vanished, out of sight. Still, that was unusual... She supposed she should investigate. It might have something to do with Antonin's disappearance, after all.

Antonin stared in horror as his last remaining weapon whizzed over the heads of his attackers and flew across the street.

He heard them start sniggering, "You really thought that would work?" One sneered at him disdainfully.

He didn't bother with a reply. There wasn't really any point.

"Well, it didn't, did it?" the man continued.

He rolled his eyes. Even when he had him cornered and was holding a gun, he was making stupid comments to try to goad him. What was the point?

He wouldn't play that game, anyway. He wasn't wasting his precious time talking when he could look for a chance - Any last chance - To get away again.

His gaze fell on a stone in the alleyway... Okay, that was a long shot and probably a stupid idea, especially after the grenade tactic had proven he couldn't throw well enough to do this.

Did he have another choice?

He dodged to the side, bending down and seizing the stone.

"Stop right there!" One of his attackers shouted at him. "I see you, plotting! You're not getting away this time. Now stay still, put your hands up!"

Cornered, Antonin dropped his new makeshift weapon. He

couldn't see any way out of this. True, they were going to shoot him anyway, he was pretty sure of that, but if he didn't provoke them, maybe another opportunity would come up...

That was how it worked in the movies, wasn't it? The hero would get a second chance. But this was real life. How likely was this to work out?

The investigation started that same day, much to Ilya's surprise. He had expected red tape and formal meetings. But he supposed this seemed more serious now that someone of his rank had been attacked in his own home, by people connected to the case Sunnikov was supposed to have handled by now.

Meeting with the investigators in his office, he explained the situation from the beginning.

"One of my officers helped on the case and has assured me he's put together sufficient evidence. Now I have more and I'm really not sure why this case isn't closed yet..." he left that sentence dangling, waiting for an answer.

The answer came crackling through his phone, which was on speaker. Sunnikov hadn't been able to attend the meeting in person due to distance, but she was quite indignant, "We're working on it!"

One of the inspectors looked sceptical, before questioning, "Why is it taking longer? With the evidence in place, the first stage of arrests should be starting..." he pointed out.

"Perhaps federal assistance is required?" Ilya suggested innocently.

"No!" Sunnikov's answer was sharp and sudden. She realised this and cleared her throat, regaining her composure. "No, that's not necessary," she added, in a calmer tone.

Another investigator cut in, "Nevertheless, this is now a federal matter. The case is clearly becoming too complicated for you to handle. You will transfer the case files to us."

Ilya heard Sunnikov's angry intake of breath. Then there was a long silence, before she admitted, "I'm afraid I can't do that..."

"Why not?!" Now the first inspector to speak did so again, sounding suspicious.

"There was a fire. We lost some files," she replied. The excuse sounded well-rehearsed, but it fell flat.

"Hm... We'll have to open an investigation then."

Ilya smiled to himself. He had won. Well, nearly... The evidence had gone. Antonin had been right about that. But while Sunnikov might have been faster than him, she wasn't going to get away with this. He sighed softly as the inspectors left his office. It was a mixed victory. He had put her in place, but she had helped the Volkovs get away with most of their crimes. And Antonin was still in danger... So was his daughter.

That thought prayed on his mind. But at least he had the new evidence from his house. He might get rid of the two attackers from the Volkov ranks, at the very least. His muddled-up thoughts were suddenly interrupted by Sunnikov, who still hadn't hung up.

"I thought I called on you to *help* me, Ilya, not make things difficult," she told him accusingly.

"Olya, you and I may be old friends, but I won't ignore corruption. I know you're on Volkov's payroll. You called me to shift the blame and now you're bitter that you failed," he answered her calmly, presenting the facts.

"That's slander, you know," she fired back, "You don't have any proof."

"And you have proof that there was a fire? Photos of the damage, records from the fire department to back you up, that kind of thing?" he suggested, suspecting she wouldn't have thought that far.

He remembered Olya Sunnikov as a clever woman, but one who thought too fast, never stopping to check that she had all her stories lined up. He hoped she hadn't changed.

There was a pause. He grinned. She hadn't changed. Her old failings were still standing in her way.

"Alright, I did it! Can you blame me for wanting just a little bit more money? The department is hardly well-funded, since we're not some huge, important city," she snapped back at him, sarcastic and annoyed, "I had the perfect plan to get all the funding I needed. If I sacrificed some pawn and sold the information to Volkov, he'd pay me pretty well. Then I could blackmail him, and he'd keep paying me..." she was ranting about her plan now, but he had tuned out.

Eventually, he heard her whine, "Ilya? Are you still there? You're not going to make trouble, are you? We're supposed to be friends..."

He shook his head, "Friends hold one another accountable. This conversation has been recorded. Goodbye, Olya." he hung up the phone as she began to yell at him and sauntered after the investigators.

He had a feeling that they would want to talk to him some more.

Oblivious to her father's successes, Nikolina was still waiting in terror for her senses to come back.

Because she knew she had to be in that alleyway. But she didn't have the courage to go in there if she was risking seeing Antonin in a dangerous situation...

She shut her eyes and tried to convince herself to go. It was only a few steps; she could do this. Then she would be with her husband again and if he was hurt or in danger, she could try her very best to help him.

Then she heard a horribly familiar sound. The chilling bang that she had heard ring out in the house echoed through the street.

Still unable to move, not daring to open her eyes, she heard footsteps running away from the scene and prayed they were Antonin's, though the pessimistic voice in her head highly doubted that that was the case.

THE END OF A LIFE

Time suddenly sped up again and Nikolina opened her eyes. Until that moment, everything seemed to have stood still from when she had heard the shot. But life poured back into her world as the frozen chill of shock was replaced with panicked realisation.

She ran into the alleyway and dropped to her knees beside her bleeding husband, tears springing to her eyes.

"No, no... Antonin!!" she yelled out desperately, her voice coming out shaky and strained as she tried to speak to him, mostly just to work out if he could hear her or not.

There was an open wound in his chest, blood spilling out. He was as white as a ghost. She squeezed her eyes shut again, not wanting to look, not wanting to believe it was real.

But it was. She had got there too late... Okay, so she couldn't have saved him, but she would rather die with him than see him like this.

He didn't manage to answer her, but stirred in her arms, making her jump. She felt for his wrist, checking for a pulse. There was something there... Perhaps she hadn't been too late after all. She could still get help for him. Except they were well away from the city hospital, he was barely alive, and she didn't have a phone on her.

The brief flicker of hope his movement had given her fought with the sense of despair she had been feeling since she had first seen the bullet in the wall at home. Things had got crazy, out of her control, but maybe she could finally do something.

Trying to pull herself together, she took deep breaths until the sobbing stopped then got to her feet and ran again, hurtling into the street and knocking on the nearest door as hard as she could.

It was still early, just getting light, and the man that opened the door was still in his pyjamas. He stood and stared at her in silence.

She could understand that. She must look pretty insane right now, with tear-stained cheeks and bedhead, dressed in her nightdress that was soaked with her husband's blood and stained with dirt from where she had fallen to the ground. Now wasn't the best time to think about that though. She had to act now.

"Please, you have to call an ambulance, my husband's been shot!!" she blurted it out, her shaky voice threatening to betray her and make her start crying again.

"Someone's been shot?!" That woke him up. He seemed incredulous now.

"Yes, in the alley... He's still alive but he needs help, quickly!" she tried to explain the situation and plead with him at the same time.

He nodded, "I'll be right back!" he ran inside, leaving her standing there.

She stood on his doorstep in the cold morning air, waiting impatiently. A few moments later, a woman emerged. She gave her a sympathetic look.

"Now, love, I know you've had a bad shock, but I'm a nurse. You need to take me to your husband, okay? I'll do what I can to keep him stable until the ambulance gets here. My husband is on the phone now." she explained gently.

Normally, Nikolina took herself very seriously and would bristle at her patronising tone. But right now, feeling as broken as she did, she took comfort in the other woman's calm, gentle demeanour. Trying to relax, she mustered a nod and led her helper back into the alleyway.

She stood well back as the nurse approached Antonin. After her initial moment with him after she found him, she was suddenly afraid to get close to him again, in case this time, her previous fear was true and there was no movement or pulse.

She couldn't do it and she knew she couldn't. She wasn't ready to lose him. She wasn't ready to accept his death. Perhaps it would have been easier if the memories of their wedding weren't still fresh in her mind, or if she wasn't pregnant with their child.

But it probably wouldn't. Regardless of all that, she loved him too much to let go.

Yet cruel fate didn't give her a choice. She remembered - Would always remember - Standing in the cold morning air and feeling the numb emptiness of heartbreak creep over her as the woman stood up and turned to face her, pale as a sheet.

"He's dead." she said bluntly.

That was it. That was all she remembered. She didn't know how she got back home that morning. She didn't know what she did that day. Her mind just kept going back to that one moment, replaying it again and again.

If it hadn't replayed so many times in her head, she probably wouldn't have believed it. How could this have happened? Antonin was young and bright, with his whole life ahead of him. He was getting on well at work and had just started a family. People like that didn't die. Death was something that happened to the old and the sick.

The whole thing seemed totally surreal to her. She didn't know how to process it. In the end, she came to a painful but necessary conclusion. Her husband had been murdered. She was in danger. Their child was in danger.

She took everything Antonin had left and stuffed it back into his big travel bag that he had only just unpacked. She packed a bag of her own as well. Everything was ready.

But, out of love and respect for her late husband, she waited until the day of the funeral. It was a small, quiet event. They didn't want to attract any unwanted guests. Herself, her family and Antonin's family - Who had flown back especially and still looked shell-shocked by the whole thing - Were the only attendees.

No one spoke to her. Her family knew she had pretty much withdrawn from the world and seemed to be respecting her decision on that, whatever they thought about it. They had the decency to let her grieve her way, though Katya kept shooting her odd looks. She did her best to ignore that.

Antonin's parents avoided her too. They seemed awkward about the whole thing. Probably because he had lived with her because they were never around. And now it was too late. Perhaps they were guilty. She would understand that. Or perhaps it was the fact that they hadn't met her before, even though she and Antonin had been married.

Whatever the reason, she had no desire to go and break the ice. For one thing, she felt awkward about the situation too. Besides, she felt watched. She had felt that way ever since his death. Perhaps she was being paranoid, but if not, she didn't want to risk putting them in danger as well.

So, the funeral took place in relative silence. It being a small event, it was over pretty quickly anyway. But she lingered at his graveside for a while afterwards, while her father walked across the graveyard, talking soberly to Antonin's parents about the legal case against his killers.

Her siblings stood around behind her awkwardly, waiting for her, but eventually, they drifted away too. She stood there a moment longer, finding it hard to leave. She had never been good at goodbyes.

Then she turned and walked away, determined to leave all this behind her, forever. It was too painful a memory and too dangerous a life.

DARIYA'S WORLD
AFTER ANTONIN

Following a little way behind the grieving family felt a little uncomfortable, as though she was stalking them, but Dariya didn't want to intrude. This was their time of grief, the last thing they needed were strangers showing up, crashing the event.

Besides, her very face meant she wasn't welcome here. She couldn't blame anyone for that. But even so, she was here because she owed it to her best friend.

She had first heard about his death when her brothers came home gloating. She had listened impassively because to cry would be to draw attention to herself. But she had slipped away while the others were celebrating and caught a train to Moscow. She felt she had to be there. So, what if they noticed her absence? At a time like this, it hardly mattered, did it?

Besides, she could always come up with a cover story. Dmitri was sure to help her. He had met her at the station, awkward in her presence because he thought she would blame him for not being able to protect Antonin. But, as she had assured him, it wasn't his fault that the rest of their family thought it was okay to murder an innocent man.

Now, she and her brother walked silently between the gravestones, lingering behind the official mourners. No one paid them any heed. Dressed all in black, they looked like they were meant to be here.

Yet, she kept her distance, not intruding. But she did glance over to Antonin's grave across the field, her eyes watering as she did. She felt Dmitri take her hand to comfort her and squeezed his hand gratefully as she shut her eyes and let the tears fall.

When she opened her eyes again, she wiped away the last of her tears with the back of her hand and tried to compose herself. It was over. Her first friendship was over and so was her first real chance at escaping the life her father had made for her. The part of her life when she had felt the most alive was over.

She blinked away fresh tears and took one last look over at Antonin's final resting place. Most of the other mourners had moved on now, but one woman lingered. She guessed this was his lover. Seeing her there was almost as heart-breaking as their loss. The poor woman had lost her husband and now she was left with an unborn child to raise and a massive target over her head.

She wondered if she ought to offer her help. She was in a difficult situation, after all, and she had promised Antonin that she would take care of his loved ones if she could.

But she faltered, her legs not wanting to move towards the other woman, and she realised she was scared, scared that she didn't fit in in this different world and scared that she wasn't welcome, that she was everything that the other would hate right now.

Not just because of her family, but because their lives were worlds apart. It had been easy to talk to Antonin, to trust him and grow close to him, in her world, on her terms. This was different. She didn't belong here.

Besides, if she was needed, Antonin had left instructions to find her. She had done what she could, or at least what she dared.

She turned to Dmitri, "We should leave..." she murmured softly.

He shrugged and walked off, pulling her with him. She realised it didn't matter to him. He was just there for her sake. But it felt harder for her to walk away, knowing what she was leaving behind her.

On the long journey back to Yaroslavl, neither she nor Dmitri said much. Her brother didn't seem to want to disturb her, and she had a lot on her mind.

For one, she was reflecting on the past. Everything that had happened with Antonin had left her even more disgusted by her father's actions than before, but it had also taken an emotional toll on her. She didn't feel like herself anymore and the constant act at home was getting harder to keep up with.

There was no question of leaving though. She would be looked for... Besides, she had an obligation. The first of the next generation of the Volkovs were beginning to be created. She wasn't their mother, not really, but they would know her as such, and she didn't feel as though she could leave them in that situation. Especially not with her father in the picture.

That led her back to her plan for rebellion and the future. She was sure that eventually, her children would be her father's downfall. She certainly hoped so. But perhaps now that he had left them with that final message, Antonin's family would play a part as well. She wondered vaguely if their children would ever meet and what they would be like...

She would do her best to guide them together into as strong a force for good as possible, but with her father giving her children 'added strengths' and the legacy of Antonin's death there to motivate his child. She wasn't entirely sure they were going to need her help. Still, she would always be there if they did.

But she knew if things got out of hand much sooner, before the next generation was ready to take on Vladimir, then she would have to turn elsewhere for allies. Of course, she had Dmitri, who had proved surprisingly loyal to her, despite their father's influence.

And perhaps Antonin's wife would seek her out. She hadn't been strong enough to reach out to the other woman that day, but if she came seeking help or even just vengeance for her husband, Dariya vowed she would be there for her. After all, neither of them had many other allies to lean on. Not now, in this world that suddenly seemed a little darker and a lot colder.

Overall, she had a lot to think about, but it didn't seem like she had enough time. Before she knew it, she was back in Yaroslavl. She walked back to the house with an increasing feeling of dread. That shouldn't happen. She was going home. But home had never been a safe place for her. Now, it was steadily becoming a nightmare.

Walking in, she could already hear the sounds of another argument. She exchanged glances with Dmitri. Tired, resigned glances. Neither of them wanted to deal with this again, but there wasn't a lot of choice.

They could run to their rooms and hide but it would be suspicious. Vladimir had already been asking awkward questions about where Dmitri had been, which was why Dariya had told him they would have to return as soon as the funeral was over. She had hoped their absence wouldn't be noticed but Vladimir noticed far too much.

So, they reluctantly slunk into the living room, trying to keep their heads down until the shouting subsided.

It didn't work. Vladimir spun around as soon as the door opened, "Where have you two been? Didn't you hear?!" he was still shouting.

Dariya sighed, "Hear what, Papa?" she asked dutifully.

"These two idiots!" he rounded on the killers.

Dariya didn't follow his gaze. Lately, she had found it hard to face her brothers without wanting to hurt them.

"These two idiots," Vladimir repeated, "left fingerprints in that Moroz guy's house. Now, he's not clever enough to get them on killing anyone, but he can prove they broke in. And this time our cop support's gone..."

Dariya bit back a smile. Antonin's death hadn't been in vain. He had got rid of one of her father's allies, narrowing it down a little more, making his life a little bit harder. She hoped her brothers would at least go to jail for a bit, though she was pretty sure her father would find another way to slither out of that.

It was something though. A small victory was enough when it was probably all she was going to get for a while.

There was a court case, and they did get convicted. Her father ranted about that for hours, even after he had got them bailed out. That wasn't the point, he said. The point was that their reputation for getting away with everything had been tarnished.

She celebrated that privately. Maybe now, if he couldn't get away with as much, her father would slip up and get into trouble. Then she could make her escape while he was out of the way.

But he was making changes, trying to ensure that that would never happen. He had already switched his workshop to another location. Not even she knew where it was now or how to get in. He kept that secret closely guarded.

She had crept into his basement to check that he actually had moved it and wasn't just trying to throw them all off the scent. But all he had underneath the house now was a set of grim little cells. Presumably, in case anyone got too close and needed disposing of in a non-lethal way. Or, knowing him, a slow way.

The other major change was that she was no longer his favourite. She had to be a little more careful herself now as he began to favour the children.

Ah, yes, the children, they were another major change. The first new clones he had successfully created and carefully aged up were alive. She had twin girls now, who were already around five because babies were 'of no use' apparently, but he could twist the minds of children.

She hated it, hated *him.* She couldn't bear to watch him with them, instead, she tried to spend her own time alone with them, undoing his lessons. It wasn't easy, with him lurking around all the time, but she had to try, after all.

The only other thing she could do was make sure that, if anything happened to her or if she couldn't speak up, there was something to tell them the truth.

Suddenly, the diaries she had promised Antonin she would write seemed more urgent. She didn't just need to commemorate the events of his case and his eventual death for his family if they ever sought the truth and she wasn't here to help them, but for her own family, so that one day, they would see through her father's lies.

The diaries were a deep, dangerous secret. If her father or anyone inclined to help him discovered them, her life would probably be over. But they were necessary too, so she couldn't avoid the situation. She just grew better and better at hiding things away from her family and lying to them.

It wasn't right, it never had been. But she didn't have a choice. Her life was on the line. Other lives had already been lost.

Sometimes you just had to lie, even to your family, because if you didn't, the bloodshed would never end.

She didn't like thinking this way. It was grim and dark. But it was the way she had been raised. Do what you have to do to survive in a world where everyone is your enemy. Her father had given her that advice in regard to helping him survive against the justice system, but now, it seemed to her, she had to survive against him instead.

Her family had become the true enemy and she had to hide from them in plain sight.

At least until such a time as she and her allies were ready to tear down Vladimir Volkovs' dark little world of lies and secrets.

NIKOLINA'S NEW LIFE

Nikolina left the night of the funeral. She left a note on the living room table, letting her family know she was safe but going into hiding. She didn't want them to worry but didn't have the courage to say goodbye in person, nor the strength to go through the inevitable argument about whether or not she should go.

Then she grabbed her bags from her room and slipped out of the house. Wandering the dark streets alone made her think of the day Antonin had died again, but she fought off the feelings. She had to stop dwelling on that and be practical if she was to avoid the same fate. The darkness would provide her with some cover if she was being watched.

Besides, she was leaving by train and the late-night trains were less crowded. The passengers were less chatty too. Whenever she used public transport, she found the strangers who thought sitting beside her and talking was a good idea annoying. She didn't have the energy to deal with them tonight.

When she reached the train station, she bought a ticket for somewhere she had never heard of before, on the basis that it was a long journey and was probably a long way out of the way. She had no other plan beyond that, but she would figure out what to do next once she was out of harm's way.

She sat in the station waiting room by herself and reached into her bag. In the side pocket was an envelope. The church had sent it to her after the wedding, with the pictures they had taken enclosed. She hadn't looked at them yet, wondering if it would be too hard.

But she supposed she would have to look at the pictures sometime. She reluctantly peeled open the envelope and took a couple of pictures out.

Staring at them, she felt tears spring to her eyes again. They could have been so happy. Despite her confusion at why he had suddenly sprung the wedding on her, that day had been the happiest of her life. Perhaps that had been the point. He had wanted to leave her with a beautiful memory.

But she wished he had told her the truth instead. It seemed so stupid that he had wasted his last hours pandering to what he thought she wanted when they could have worked out some plan to save him.

Hurt by her own emotional thoughts, Nikolina pulled the pictures out of the envelope and ripped them into pieces, before chucking the tattered remains into the nearest bin. What was the point in keeping something that was meant to be beautiful if all it did was make her cry?

She sat back down and took out the *other* envelope, the one Antonin had left. She had found it with his things. It had been on top of the music books he had left in her room. It was addressed to her, so she supposed it was about time she read it.

Opening it up, she read it slowly and carefully, going back through it a couple of times to make sure she had understood it properly.

She had to check because she had never been very musical, but it seemed to be a love song. She didn't know whether to smile or cry. He had been learning more music recently and had promised that when he got the hang of it, he would write a love song for her. He'd said he would play it on his guitar and sing for her.

She had been looking forward to that, but then he became busier and busier at work and... Still somehow found time to finish it, but never had a chance to sing it.

Fresh tears fell and this time, she didn't have it in her to destroy the cause of them. She folded it up instead and opened one of Antonin's old music books, carefully slotting the sheet of music inside.

As she did so, she spotted something else on the floor and grabbed it, assuming it had fallen from the envelope too. She couldn't bring herself to look at anything else that might make her cry, so she stuffed into the book with the song.

Shutting the book, she shoved it back into her bag. That was enough memories and enough emotions. She had to learn to compose herself perfectly from now on and give nothing away about her grief, lest her husband's murders use it against her.

The train soon arrived, and she left on it. The journey was long, and she fell asleep a few times on the train, but at the very end of the journey, she stepped out and looked around.

Well, she was somewhere new, ready to start a new life whether she wanted to or not. But now what?

She had to find somewhere to stay, to start with. She had been prepared for that, though, and taken some money out of her bank account to make sure she could pay for decent accommodation. It would have to be suitable for her and her future child to live comfortably, after all.

Then she wasn't sure what would come next. Finding a job here, probably. But she hadn't considered that before, so she had never officially left her other job.

Of course, there was no question of going back to it. Either her father would inform her boss of what she had done, or she would just stop turning up and eventually would be fired. That was a shame, it had been a good job and she had just found her feet there.

Still, there would be other jobs, wouldn't there? It wasn't the end of the world, she told herself. She would have to learn to put all the attachments of her old life behind her and move on without getting emotional.

She tried to convince herself it was for the best as she walked away from the station, off to start her new life.

It took her a few months to properly establish herself again. She rented a small, one-bedroom flat in the outskirts of the town she had landed in and for a while, she just stayed there, out of the way, keeping herself to herself.

Then she had to address the employment issue, as money began to run low. It wasn't easy. By that point, she was noticeably pregnant and that seemed to put off potential employers.

But she managed to find something, eventually. It was a menial shelf-stacking job at the town's only supermarket, nothing like as challenging as her previous job. But it allowed her to keep paying rent and providing for herself, so she took it.

She was able to save some extra money, which she vowed she would use to provide for her child as well when the time came.

That was the only important thing right now. She didn't bother talking to her co-workers much, leaving them to gossip about her being 'stuck-up'. She didn't care. She just wanted a quiet life in which she and her child would be safe, and the past would be left behind her.

So that was how she lived until one night, she went into labour. After a few hours, she found herself holding her daughter and feeling overwhelmed.

There were too many emotions running around her head for her to process right now. She was happy, of course, to finally meet her baby. But she was hurting too. Holding her and Antonin's baby in her arms, she looked down and couldn't help but think of him. It was a bittersweet moment.

There was also a hint of fear that was only growing stronger as she looked at her daughter. This child was so tiny, so fragile... And she was already in grave danger. She had been born in danger and may never escape it. And she couldn't even protect herself.

Nikolina didn't know how she was going to protect this precious, helpless little life. She was doing what she thought was best, but she was all on her own and had to look after not only herself but the baby as well.

The panic suddenly gripped her. What was she going to do? How could she do this? She couldn't! She couldn't do it alone!!

Out of the panic rose one calm, clear thought. Then go home.

She bit her lip. Could she go back home? Her family would welcome her, and she knew that they would do everything they could to help her. But wouldn't she be putting them in danger too?

No, because they already *were* in danger, she reminded herself. They had been since the break-in, yet none of them had tried to run from it or hide away. They faced it calmly. Together.

They said there was strength in numbers, after all. And then, if something did happen, her baby would have a family to look after her. Here, she had nobody but Nikolina, who was rapidly getting less and less confident that she could do anything useful.

She was out of her depth here. She had to go home.

HIDING THE PAST

Nikolina left town as soon as she had recovered from the birth of Nadezhda, her young daughter.

She caught another train and went home. It felt strange repeating the journey again, this time holding Nadezhda in her arms and trying to soothe away the child's cries.

Not as weird as it seemed at the end of the journey, though, when she had to leave the train and trek back home. It seemed surreal, standing outside her family home and wondering how she would be received when she entered.

She knew they would welcome her home, of course. But how would she answer their questions? She had disappeared for nine months and now she was showing up on their doorstep with a baby in her arms.

She had never even told her family members that she was pregnant. How was she going to handle this?

There were two options that came to mind: She could tell them the truth, with all its uncomfortable emotions. That would be hard for her and it might also put her daughter in danger. If she shared her true identity with anyone, it could leak out and back to the Volkovs.

Maybe she was being paranoid there, but she couldn't bear the idea of her baby being hurt. That was why she hadn't put Antonin's name on her birth certificate. She hadn't mentioned him at all.

So, she wasn't being entirely truthful, but the second option would take that much further. She could actively lie about her daughter's life. If no one except her knew that Antonin was Nadezhda's father, then the danger would be... Not gone but minimised at least.

But how would she do that? She needed to get her story straight and tell everyone the same thing. And it had to be plausible. But she had never had another partner besides Antonin, so how would she make this convincing?

... Adoption! She could tell people she had been away to adopt Nadezhda. That would make sense. She nodded to herself. Alright, that would be the plan then. Time to put it into action.

She strode up to the door, trying to appear confident in spite of her nerves. Banging on the front door, she waited for a response.

Ilya answered. He opened the door calmly and then stared at her for a few moments. "Nikolina? You're back!" he smiled and moved to hug her before noticing the baby in her arms.

"Umm..." he didn't seem to know what to say. There was an awkward pause.

She tried to find the words to begin the lie. "Well, yes, I am back. And very, very glad to be!" she added honestly, "But I suppose I ought to explain. I have adopted, this is Nadezhda," she held up the baby.

Ilya looked down at his grandchild and smiled, "Lovely, Lina, but do you think I'm stupid?" he was suddenly serious again.

That threw her, "What? Of course not!" she spluttered.

"Then don't lie to me. Adopted?" he raised an eyebrow, "I don't believe that," he saw her panicked face and sighed, "It's fine, I understand. Come in and we can talk about it better."

Well, I'm clearly a terrible liar, Nikolina thought to herself as she followed him into the house. At least he didn't seem mad about it. Maybe he would help her come up with a better plan for keeping her daughter safe.

She dragged her bags in as well and dumped them in the hall, before trailing after her father again. Soon, she found herself sitting opposite him at the dinner table.

"Well, whatever you need to explain, go ahead," he told her, sitting back and waiting patiently, his expression impassive.

Nikolina nodded, "Antonin and I found out we were having a

baby the day that we got married. I thought I would wait to share the news when things were a little more settled and then when he died... I couldn't stay here. I felt as though I was in danger too and I was putting her in danger by staying. I don't trust those Volkov people to stay away... You haven't heard any more from them, have you?" she trailed off from her explanation to question him suspiciously.

"No, not since I made sure those two who broke in went to jail... But I think you're right not to trust them," he nodded.

"What to do you suggest I do about it then? Because I have tried so hard and all I have learnt is that I can't handle this alone!" she felt close to panic again as she threw those words at him.

Ilya shook his head, "I know. I don't think any of us can. That's why I've arranged police protection for us, just to be sure. I'll extend it to you and Nadya as well. Keeping her safe will have to be a priority. No doubt she'll be the number one target if they learn of her existence," he explained.

Nikolina nodded in agreement, "That is probably wise. Thank you," she smiled slightly, glad of his help. "Is there anything else that we can do to keep her safe?" she asked, still anxious.

"Hm..." he considered the question carefully, "Well, we should probably continue your plan and lie about her identity. The truth can be very dangerous. No one else should know, not even Sasha and Katya."

He sounded very grave, and she nodded, understanding, "I know. But obviously, I am a rotten liar, how are we going to get them to believe all this?"

"I'll back you up, of course," he assured her.

And so, with her father's help, Nikolina settled back into her old life.

Ilya helped her with everything. He gave her back her old room until she found somewhere else to live, he helped her get her former job back and helped out with childcare when he could.

And, as promised, he helped explain her return and her new child to her siblings. Somehow, he made them accept it. He even tried to convince them that she had never been truly in love with Antonin, and that his death had put them all in danger because he had betrayed them while he was away on his mission. Henceforth, the Moroz siblings stopped speaking of him. They stopped visiting his grave. They began to forget him. Nikolina never did, of course, but she pretended to. Though she wasn't entirely sure that her siblings believed the united act of herself and her father. Well, Sasha seemed to take it in his stride. But Katya, certainly, was behaving oddly towards her.

But she ignored the brewing tension between herself and her sister, hoping it would come to nothing. She was just glad to be back with her family, all safe and sound.

She was grateful to her father for arranging protection for them. A part of her was still living in fear. But life did move on and with it, hope for a better future trickled into her life.

Mostly it came through changes. She got her old job back and worked hard for a promotion. She saved up her money and got a home for herself and Nadezhda. Living in her old room with a new baby and all the things she needed to care for her was getting hard.

She wouldn't have swapped it for another life though, even when it was painful to deal with the similarities between her deceased husband and her growing daughter. She still struggled to handle the grief of losing Antonin in any other way than shutting away her emotions completely, but Nadezhda helped her to feel better and to have hope.

She kept an emotional distance between her and her daughter, not wanting to get too close, only to lose her, but she already felt a deep attachment to the child and every day with her made her hopeful.

This little girl who seemed so carefree and so joyous might be tiny and helpless now, but who knew what she could grow up to achieve?

Sometimes, when her daughter laughed - Which she seemed to do a lot - It felt like she could do anything, change anyone's heart for the better and even change the whole world.

She was being silly; she knew she was. It was the sentimental stupidity of a loving mother. There was nothing in it. But she needed thoughts like that to help her push away her other feelings and get through the day without breaking down into tears.

So, she would always speculate on the hopeful future, rather than the grim past.

That dark time, though it was not that long ago, was too much for her. She had to shut it out almost entirely to cope with it. And to keep safe. If she mentioned it to anyone, even in passing, she could be putting herself and her whole family in danger. Especially Nadezhda.

So, she hid away the memories. She kept Antonin's old belongings blended in with hers around the house, so they wouldn't draw attention like they might if she suddenly got a skip and threw them all away,

But his old things were the only reminders of the dark past

- Besides her daughter's resemblance to him - That she kept around.

She hoped that she had done enough to make the Volkovs forget about her and her family. And to make herself forget about the most painful part of her life.

She should have done. She had run, hidden and lied. She had got help and protection around her.

So that hopefully, her daughter would never have to suffer like this. She would never even have to know about it.

BOOKS IN THIS SERIES

The Secrets Series

The Secrets Series spans across over twenty years as one family spend generations trying to break a city free from the sinister grasp of a powerful Russian mafia family with twisted secrets to hide and dark plans. Who will triumph, and at what cost?

Secrets Of The Volkovs

Disappearances, deaths, threats... The local police are beginning to suspect all these crimes are linked. They're being committed by the sinister and mysterious Volkov family.

There's just one problem: They can't prove it. In order to take down the Volkovs and put a stop to these crimes, they call in a young, ambitious policeman, Antonin Jelennski.

Antonin travels hundreds of miles, leaving his fiancee behind, to go undercover and infiltrate the Volkovs' organisation. He pins down incriminating evidence, but he finds far more than they ever expected. Can he expose the dark secrets of the Volkovs and stop their crimes before it's too late?

Family Secrets

'The discovery was a complete accident, of course. Nadezhda never set out to make an enemy of the woman she believed to be her adoptive mother.'

When Nadezhda Moroz finds a photo of her adoptive mother and realises she's been living a lie, she ignores all warnings from her family and sets out to discover the grisly secret that killed her father just days after his wedding...

What she finds reveals just how twisted up her family's history is. Her search for the truth pushes her into the arms of the mysterious Vasily Volkov, who promises he knows her story...

And his strange, sinister family, who seem to have other secrets on their minds. The family seems to operate like a mafia group, and before long, Nadezhda is helplessly entangled with them, trapped in the town they appear to control. She meets old and new allies while in their clutches and escapes with her allies to bring them to justice, risking her life to fight them

Secrets In The Flames

Nadezhda Moroz has spent the last five years trying to put her encounter with the evil Volkov mafia behind her. She faced them at just sixteen, trying to avenge their murder of her father. But now, the ringleaders are behind bars and she is free to enjoy her uncle's wedding. Or is she?

An uninvited guest serves as a reminder that it's never that easy to walk away from the past. Her one-time boyfriend turned enemy with an obsessive vendetta has taken control of the local prison and is using his newfound power to endanger thousands of lives.

Desperate to stop him, Nadezhda teams up with friends, family and old enemies. She has no choice but to trust them all with her life as they face war. But she doesn't know what she's dealing with. Her nemesis has a dark secret, with which he plans to destroy her and everyone she holds dear.

Printed in Great Britain
by Amazon

15987098R00102